Presented in honor of your
outstanding achievement in the
Arts & Writing Contest of the

HOLOCAUST EDUCATION &
RESOURCE CENTER
OF
RHODE ISLAND

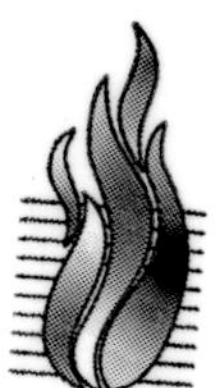

By the Dr. Alfred Jaffe
Endowment Fund

Ordinary People, Turbulent Times

Alice Dreifuss Goldstein

AuthorHouse™
1663 Liberty Drive, Suite 200
Bloomington, IN 47403
www.authorhouse.com
Phone: 1-800-839-8640

First published by AuthorHouse 7/21/2008

ISBN: 978-1-4343-8122-4 (sc)

Library of Congress Control Number: 2008903772

Printed in the United States of America
Bloomington, Indiana

This book is printed on acid-free paper.

In memory of my grandparents

Ludwig and Karolina Dreifuss
and
Sigmund and Anna Valfer

whose faith and love helped them survive many turbulent years and helped to shape my future

Acknowledgments

I am most thankful to the Holocaust Education and Resource Center of Rhode Island for providing the context within which I was able to find my voice and develop my story. Their continued support and interest have been invaluable. I am indebted to Reinhardt Haemmerle, Robert Krais, and Annegrete Kessler of the *Deutsch Israelischer Arbeitskreis* for the work they are doing to keep alive the memory of southwest Germany's Jews and for all their assistance during my visits to Kenzingen and Freiburg. Many thanks to Doris Donovan, Herman Goldstein, Anneliese Greenier, and Eleanor Lewis for their insightful comments on drafts of the manuscript. Special thanks to David Lewis for his patience and expertise in preparing the photos for publication. I am especially grateful to my husband, Sidney Goldstein, whose positive critical reviews and continued encouragement have helped to bring this project to completion. Our three children and seven grandchildren have heard of my past often; putting those stories into more permanent form reflects my deep love for them all.

Alice Goldstein
Rhode Island 2008

Table of Contents

Preface

I love to tell stories. So it was natural for me to tell some of my family stories to my children and grandchildren. Those stories and memories evolved with a different focus as I became a speaker for the RI Holocaust Education and Resource Center. Since the 1980s, I have shared various parts of my family history with teens and adults seeking a better understanding of the sequence of events in 1930s Nazi Germany that served as a prelude to the Shoah. These presentations have helped me to organize our family history and have also forced me to think in considerable depth not only about the turmoil of events in which we were caught up, but also about the intangibles – feelings at the time, reactions, and personal impacts later in life. Teenagers often ask the most searching questions; trying to answer them honestly has enriched my own awareness of my heritage.

In giving these presentations, I have drawn on many sources. Foremost is my own memory, both of the stories I heard from my parents as a child and of my own experiences growing up in Kenzingen, Germany. Since I fled Germany when I was only eight years old, I often questioned the accuracy of my memories. They were corroborated and augmented some 62 years later. In 2001, under the auspices of the *Deutsch Israelischer Arbeitskreis* (German Israelite Work Group), I returned to Kenzingen for the first time since 1939, to meet with residents who knew my family and who could add to my memories of those early years.

Fortunately, I also have many documents that my father retained, including correspondence which related to our emigration, affidavits he and others in the family had to provide to Nazi authorities, and the paperwork involved in attempts to obtain authorization to allow my grandparents to emigrate to the United States. As part of their emigration process, my parents also made sure to pack official documents related to births and marriage, school records, and work recommendations. Once in the United States, my parents also kept the letters and envelopes that arrived from relatives still in Germany, and especially from my grandparents before and after they were deported from their homes. These primary sources have been invaluable in filling out the details of my family's history.

That I know anything about the early history of the Dreifuss family is the result of a serendipitous coincidence. As part of my work toward a Master's degree in history, I undertook a demographic analysis of a German *Ortsippenbuch* (Genealogy book) for the town of Altdorf, Baden, which happened to be my ancestors' initial place of settlement in Germany. That research allowed me to reconstruct the life of Jews, including my family, in the 18th and early 19th centuries.

In response to my talks in schools, I have also read broadly to be able to provide the general historical context against which my story played out. Especially, I have tried to place my family's experiences within the larger scope of world history in order to show its relevance to problems at the beginning of the 21st century. My purpose is to raise young peoples' awareness of human rights and civil liberties, and the need to be vigilant in their defense. This is also the goal of this written account, aimed at those young people who embody our future.

Alice Goldstein
Warwick, Rhode Island, 2008

Ordinary People, Turbulent Times

Endings and Beginnings

Saturday, August 26, 1939: The world is mobilizing for war. Germany threatens Poland; Poles "are in a state of full readiness"; Louvre treasures are ordered moved into storage for safekeeping; Bermuda declares martial law; children are being evacuated from London to safety in the British countryside. World leaders make desperate attempts to forestall armed conflict. *The New York Times* banner headline across all columns of page 1 declares: Hitler Reported Willing to Ease Demands on Poland ... Roosevelt Addresses New Peace Appeal to Germany. FDR fervently hopes that peaceful solutions can be found to Hitler's demands for the Danzig corridor (part of Poland in 1939) and that the deaths of thousands through war can be averted. Nonetheless, a German warship has steamed into Danzig harbor amid the cheers of the residents.

Sunday sermons announced for the following day are focusing on prayers for peace. That Saturday's sermons in the synagogues seem somewhat more realistic: "The War of Nerves," "Farewell to Peace," and "The Red Front."

Meanwhile, life in the United States is quite normal. Socialites are still going to Newport for the summer air. The World's Fair in New York is in full swing, despite the low attendance the previous day due to heavy rains; some 19 million tickets have already been sold. The Yankees have won both games in a double header against the St. Louis Browns and are 3 games ahead of Boston in the American League standings. The 25 millionth automobile is clocked going over the

Henry Hudson Bridge. Movie theaters are featuring "Goodbye Mr. Chips," "The Conquest of Peter the Great" (with an ad comment of "Oh so timely"!); Radio City Music Hall is showing "Fifth Avenue Girl" with Ginger Rogers; and "The Wizard of Oz" is in its first run at the Capitol Theater (Mickey Rooney and Judy Garland perform live on stage after the movie). The theater has a full season of shows, including "The George White Scandals," "Tobacco Road," "Philadelphia Story," starring Katharine Hepburn, and "Little Foxes" with Tallulah Bankhead. The radio features many classical music programs, but also several reports on the situation in Europe, the Red Skelton comedy show, and the Goodman orchestra.

Perhaps because of the experiences of World War I, with memories of the Lusitania still strong, leaders are expressing considerable concern about maritime traffic. "War clouds bring chaos on the sea," opines the *Times*, which also prints maps showing the locations of passenger liners. Americans are rushing to book passage leaving Europe amid the cancellation of many sailings and the delays of others. The society pages note the arrival that Saturday of the USS Harding, because on board were several men of note: Capt. Fred Lawton, the skipper of the Vanderbilt yacht; Sir Raymond Unwin, a British architect; and H.R. Elkins, Rome manager for United Press, recently expelled from Italy (for anti-fascist comments? because he is Jewish?).

Also on board in third class, but of no interest whatsoever to the *NY Times*, are the Dreifusses -- Siegfried, Gretel, and me, their seven year old daughter, Alice. We are among the many passengers – Jewish refugees from Europe – who are seeking safe haven in America. Our day began just as dawn was beginning to throw some light through the cloudy sky. Gretel (Mama) came into the stateroom and reached into the upper berth to shake my shoulder and wake me up. "Get dressed and come on deck with me," she urged. I grumbled and burrowed under the blanket to go back to sleep. But Mama persisted, and I grudgingly climbed out of the berth and into my clothes. We rushed upstairs to join the crowd of passengers lining the rails of the USS Harding and staring over the water. There, just becoming visible, stood the Statue of Liberty to greet us as we sailed to safety.

As an eight year old, I certainly wasn't aware of the full significance of that hour, but I can now easily imagine with what mixed feelings we greeted the sight of New York harbor and its symbol of welcome. We had finally reached the end of our flight from Nazi Germany. The week aboard ship was without specific responsibilities or dangers. Worry and sorrow about loved ones still in Hitler's Germany and acute concern over the future in America sailed with us across the Atlantic. But the ship also provided a respite and contrast to the tensions and restrictions left behind.

Once we docked, the reality of our situation closed in. We were in a strange land where a foreign language was spoken, where Papa had no work, where we had few contacts. Fortunately, the paper work of getting us out of the ship and onto the docks went smoothly. We saw for the first time the opulence of first class, since that's where customs and immigration officials set up their tables. I was so impressed by the chandeliers and broad staircase. Some official stamps, a close look at our health certificates, and a "Welcome to the United States" completed the formalities. Once on the dock, we found Cousin Ilse (now an Americanized Elsie), who quickly took charge and whisked us into the bewildering world of New York City, our new home.

As two decades of world peace came to a close and nations girded for conflict, a new life began for us, and my family's long history in rural Germany ended.

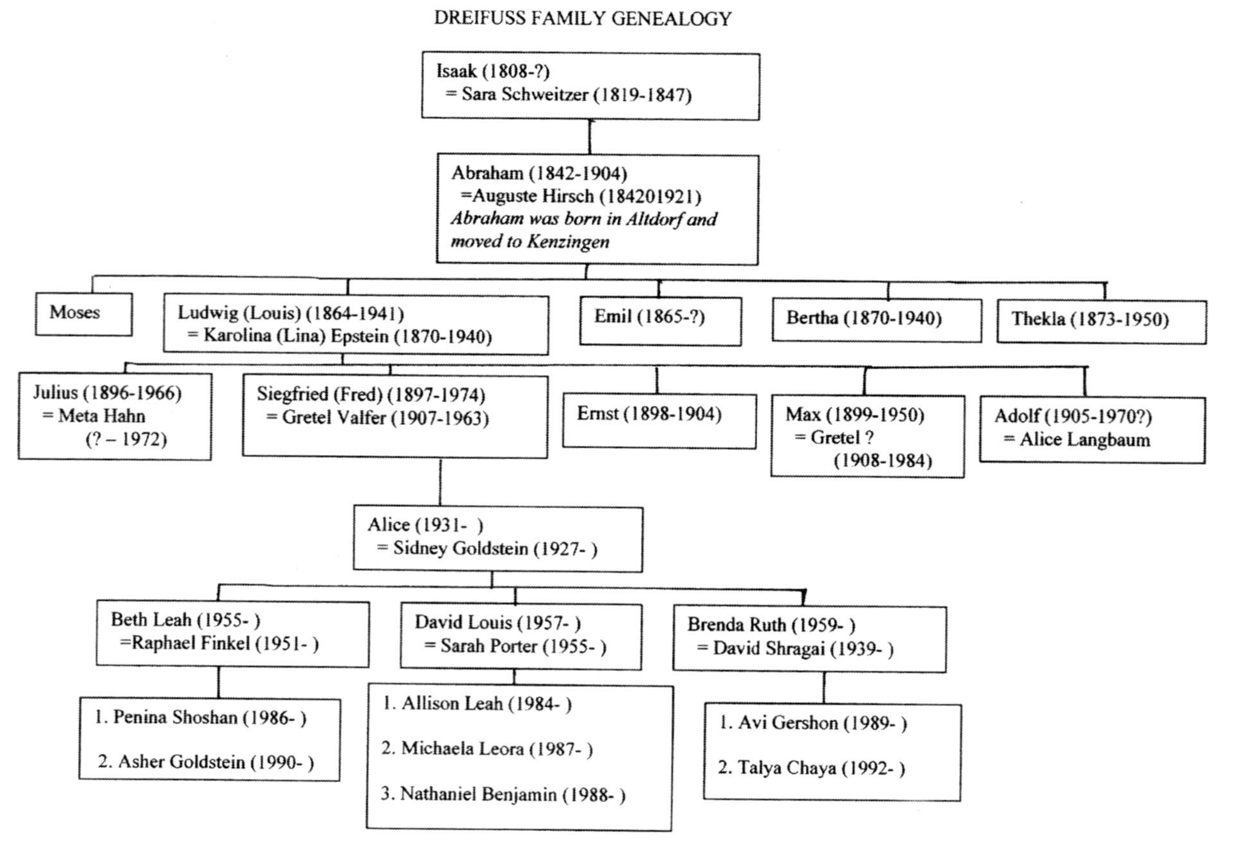
DREIFUSS FAMILY GENEALOGY
Isaak (1808-?)
= Sara Schweitzer (1819-1847)
Abraham (1842-1904)
=Auguste Hirsch (184201921)
Abraham was born in Altdorf and moved to Kenzingen
Moses
Ludwig (Louis) (1864-1941)
= Karolina (Lina) Epstein (1870-1940)
Emil (1865-?)
Bertha (1870-1940)
Thekla (1873-1950)
Julius (1896-1966)
= Meta Hahn
(? – 1972)
Siegfried (Fred) (1897-1974)
= Gretel Valfer (1907-1963)
Ernst (1898-1904)
Max (1899-1950)
= Gretel ?
(1908-1984)
Adolf (1905-1970?)
= Alice Langbaum
Alice (1931-)
= Sidney Goldstein (1927-)
Beth Leah (1955-)
=Raphael Finkel (1951-)
David Louis (1957-)
= Sarah Porter (1955-)
Brenda Ruth (1959-)
= David Shragai (1939-)
1. Penina Shoshan (1986-)
2. Asher Goldstein (1990-)
1. Allison Leah (1984-)
2. Michaela Leora (1987-)
3. Nathaniel Benjamin (1988-)
1. Avi Gershon (1989-)
2. Talya Chaya (1992-)

Rural Origins and Town Destinations

My ancestors originated in Alsace – a province in the northeast of France, as did many of the Jews who populated the small towns and villages of Southwest Germany, land of the Black Forest, Grimm fairy tales, and cuckoo clocks. They crossed the Rhine from France in the early eighteenth century and went into the small lands held by bishops or margraves who were willing to let Jews settle in their territory. The Jews brought with them not only their faith in Judaism and their skills and networks, but also a predilection for the foods favored in Alsace and a smattering of French vocabulary. For example, a favorite food was sauerkraut cooked with sautéed onions and wine. And the newcomers referred to the sidewalk not as *Gehweg* or *Buergerstein* as proper Germans would, but as *trottoir.*

The period was one of considerable instability and uncertainty for Jews and non-Jews alike. For centuries, the area had been a crossroad for the armies of Europe, as one group or another swept first east, then west. Allegiance to various rulers shifted often and invariably brought new taxes and new laws. It was not until the period around the French Revolution that territorial and legal jurisdiction was stabilized. During their early period, the Jews in the area of the Black Forest were terribly poor; most men roamed the countryside as peddlers and were often prohibited from dealing with non-Jews. Because these peddlers continued to adhere to their Jewish practices, especially *kashrut* (the dietary laws) and the prohibition against work on the Sabbath, inns run by Jews for Jews sprang up throughout the area. The inns often formed the nucleus of a growing Jewish community. My ancestors eventually settled in Altdorf, where a sizable Jewish community developed, but even there Jewish poverty remained acute during the eighteenth century.

Toward the end of the eighteenth century, profound economic changes occurred. Peasants increasingly turned to cattle raising and growing maize and hay to provide fodder for their livestock; some of the more traditional agricultural crops were abandoned. The fields and slopes of the area around the Black Forest were well suited to these new pursuits. The population of the region grew, and as villages and towns expanded, all sorts of opportunities arose for skilled workers and service providers. Many of these needs were filled by the local people, but others were more suited for the Jewish in-migrants.

The tolerant attitudes of the local ruler (Karl Friedrich, the Margrave of Baden) allowed Jews to learn trades and most crafts. Many Jews became butchers, bakers, or shop keepers. Since they were not allowed to own agricultural land, village-based work enabled them to make a living without engaging directly in farming. Most prominently, many became closely involved in the cattle trade. Jews came to serve as the middle men between the peasants who raised the cattle and the wholesalers who slaughtered the beasts and sold the meat. The Jewish cattle dealers bought the cattle from their peasant neighbors and took them to market for resale. In the process, Jews assumed the risk of the final sale and lowered the risk for the peasants in the villages. The wide connections with fellow religionists in the area helped Jews to develop networks that facilitated their trade. Both Christians and Jews prospered under this arrangement, and it was not until well into the twentieth century that non-Jews also proliferated among cattle dealers. By then, however, cattle-dealing had become so heavily a Jewish occupation, carried on in a Yiddish dialect unique to it, that a dictionary was compiled of Yiddish/German specifically for cattle dealers.

Jews felt quite comfortable in the villages and often, by the middle of the nineteenth century, in places like Altdorf, came to constitute as much as one-fifth of the population. In other places in the region, like Kenzingen, only a few families settled. Where there was a sizable number of Jews, cemetery land was purchased, a synagogue might be built, religious education was provided, and shops sprang up to cater to a Jewish clientele. Jewish inns continued to be welcome, since many Jews in the early decades of the nineteenth century still peddled their goods over a large area and often had to stay away from home for days at a time. Altdorf had such an inn, and also its own synagogue, although trained rabbis served the community only sporadically.

The cemetery for Altdorf's Jews was located in Schmieheim, some 3 kilometers distant. It occupied a grassy slope amid fields and small woods and was truly a place of peace. To reach it, the Jews of Altdorf walked along a narrow tree-lined road that curved along the side of a hill. In a funeral procession, the coffin was often carried the entire distance on the shoulders of a few men, although sometimes a cart was used.

On the whole, Jews lived amicably with their neighbors, although they were often the subject of special taxes or laws designed to make them more German and thereby ostensibly improve their status. For example, Jews traditionally had a given name and designated "the son of...," but in the mid-19th century, all had to adopt surnames. Elementary education, even though taught in Jewish schools (*Jüdische Volkschule*) included a mandatory secular curriculum; secondary education was also available in Jewish schools, but in many communities, Jewish youth opted for the secular schools. In appearance and housing, there was little to distinguish Jews from their Christian neighbors, and, indeed, in Altdorf, Jews lived throughout the town, rather than in a single "Jewish section."

Nonetheless, they remained distinct in their observance of the Sabbath and holidays and of *kashrut,* and Hebrew/Yiddish words were an important part of their vocabulary. In the summer, they might complain of the *chamimeh* – a corruption of the Hebrew word for hot, *cham*; and they were very sensitive to *risches* (from the Hebrew *rasch*) – anti-semitism.

The Jews in this corner of Germany were little affected by the reform movements that swept Jewish congregations in the larger cities to the north and east. Their religion was a combination of tradition and elements borrowed from the popular culture; it contained few elements of dedicated learning or scholarship. Some have termed it a "folk religion." For example, in the High Holy Day liturgy, the melodies sung by the cantor often included snippets from opera; the "Last Rose of Summer" was a popular tune for prayers. The Altdorf synagogue, built in the middle of the nineteenth century, stood on a corner near the center of town. Like most of the buildings around it, it had a stucco façade and a tiled roof. The interior included a small foyer, with steps leading up to the women's gallery. The town's *mikveh* (ritual bath) served Altdorf and the surrounding area, as did the kosher butcher and the *matzoh* bakery.

Abraham Dreifus was the first member of our family to be on record as living in Altdorf. He moved there with his wife, Dosel Weil. We know very little about their life before they settled in Altdorf, or even when they moved there. We do know that their first child was born in 1799, and that over the next two decades a total of four daughters and four sons were born to the couple. Abraham was a cattle dealer, as were two of his sons, Isaak and Jakob. The other sons, Samuel and Simon, were small shopkeepers or traders. Two of the daughters were on record as marrying, Babette to a local man, Franziska to someone from a nearby town --Rust. We don't know what happened to Blümel and Theila. Isaak, Samuel, and Jakob all married women from Altdorf.

Isaak was married twice. His first marriage, to Sara Schweitzer, took place in 1838. Over the next decade, Sara bore 5 children, two of whom (Fanny and Emanuel) died in infancy. Dusette seems to have left Altdorf before marrying, and Sophie died at an early age, 25, before she had a chance to marry. Only Abraham married within the town. Sara herself died in 1847, only a year and a half after giving birth to her last child. Since Isaak was still relatively young, he remarried a year after Sara died. His new wife, Rosina Bernheimer, bore 9 children, including twins. Four of the children died in infancy or childhood; the remainder moved from Altdorf.

According to the records we have, then, of Isaak's 14 children, only Abraham married within the town. We don't know with certainty why so many of Isaak's children moved from Altdorf, but we can make some educated guesses. Altdorf was a growing town in the middle of the nineteenth century, but it certainly could not have supported all the offspring of the prolific Jewish families -- or of the families of their

Catholic fellow townspeople. The Catholics could remain in the area by expanding land under cultivation or for use as grazing grounds. New crops, like tobacco were introduced, which further expanded opportunities for the growing population. But Jews could not own land and could not turn to similar solutions. Out-migration thus became a useful solution for the Jews. They had connections in many other places in the region, both family and business; many had also had experiences out of Altdorf, because they had often been sent away to serve as apprentices or to otherwise further their education. There was little to keep them in Altdorf or to lure them back once they had been to the region's cities.

Abraham followed the trend. Although born and schooled in Altdorf, and married there in June 1863, he left to resettle in Kenzingen in 1861. He seems to have dabbled in real estate, buying and selling several houses before buying a three-storey house at No. 6 Brotstrasse. There he established a general household goods store, which served an important niche in the general village economy. Having established himself at last, he felt ready to return to Altdor for his bride Auguste Hirsch, who had also been born in Altdorf in 1842, and bring her to their new household in Kenzingen. By the time the couple began having children, they were established in their new village.

Kenzingen Genesis: My Father's Family

Kenzingen is situated not far from Altdorf, within a few kilometers of the Rhine River on one side, and the Black Forest on the other. It is tucked into rolling hills and green meadows, excellent locations for the small farming and orchards, cattle raising, and tobacco cultivation that occupied the peasantry. Unfortunately for the village, as for many others in the region, it lay in a most strategic area, where France, Germany, and Switzerland met. Armies swept across the area with great regularity, from the medieval period right through the Napoleonic Wars and beyond. Like Altdorf, the village came under the governance of a variety of rulers, but it held fast to its Catholic faith and, eventually, its German nationality.

Unlike Altdorf, Kenzingen failed to experience a spurt of growth in the eighteenth or early nineteenth centuries. The narrow cobbled streets and half-timbered houses with their red tile roofs remained stolidly in place, with few new houses being built. Farmers went out daily to their fields, and when they returned in the evening, watered their cattle at one of the many drinking troughs scattered throughout the village. The village centered on the Catholic church and its open courtyard, and boasted a small hospital run by an order of nuns.

Dreifuss family store and house, Brotstrasse, Kenzingen, 1905

When Abraham Dreifuss arrived in the village, he undoubtedly had little capital and few connections there. Only a handful of Jewish families were resident. But he apparently saw it as a place of opportunity. He began by buying a house (Jews were forbidden to buy agricultural land outside the village), which he soon sold for a different one. Eventually he bought a three story building on Brotstrasse and established a dry goods shop on the ground floor. The building was well-suited to raising a family since it had enough space for the store and four rooms on each of the other two floors, plus a generous balcony in the rear, a small enclosed back courtyard, and a barn.

Auguste and Abraham had five children. They grew up in Kenzingen, but only two, Ludwig and Bertha remained there into adulthood. The others moved to neighboring towns. Ludwig (Louis) grew into a dashing young man with a handlebar moustache, but his hair thinned rather early in life. He married Karolina (Lina) Epstein a beautiful, blond, blue-eyed young woman from Eichstetten, a nearby regional town. She was the sister of one of the few other Jewish householders in the village. Lina's family had been living in various villages and towns of Baden since the early eighteenth century, and counted among their forebears cantors and other leaders of the Jewish community. Her own immediate family was of moderate means, dealing in animal fodder and grains.

Engagement picture of Ludwig (Louis) Dreifuss, c. 1894

Engagement picture of Karolina (Lina) Epstein, c. 1894

Although Louis and Lina remained in Kenzingen, they maintained contacts with family members in other locations in the area, particularly family in Altdorf and those who had settled in the somewhat larger town of Emmendingen. These contacts were important since any religious contacts outside the home would have had to have been elsewhere; Kenzingen had no Jewish institutions at all. While both Altdorf and Emendingen had synagogues, the main cemetery for Jews in the area was in Schmieheim, where Abraham and Auguste (Louis' parents) were buried.

Siegfried Dreifuss with his Grandmother Epstein, 1901

Lina bore five sons to Ludwig. The oldest, Julius, was born in 1896, and was followed a year later by my father, Siegfried. A third son, Ernst, was born in 1898, and Adolf in 1899. The four boys all survived their early years, but an outbreak of scarlet fever in 1904 swept through the family and took the life of the six year old. A year later, perhaps to compensate for the lost son, a final child, Max, completed the family. The four boys grew up in the village along with their non-Jewish peers. Since they were among the few Jewish children in Kenzingen, most of their friends were Catholic. Yet they were barely regarded as different and seemed fully comfortable participating in a variety of school activities, dramatics, glee club, and sports.

The four Dreifuss brothers, standing left to right: Siegfried, Julius, Max; seated: Adolf 1908

As the boys grew into adulthood, it seemed clear that the store could generate a livelihood for only one additional family. Both Julius and Max were interested in leaving the village for a more exciting life in the city. In this they followed a pattern very common among Jews throughout the hamlets of southwest Germany. By the end of the nineteenth century, young Jews had begun to desert the villages and flock to the larger cities of the area, especially Freiburg, Karlsruhe, and Mannheim, but also the more distant cities of Germany, like Frankfurt and Berlin. By the end of the first decade of the twentieth century, only Siegfried was interested in remaining at home to inherit the family business. (Adolf was still too young at this point to be considered.) In 1913, Siegfried was therefore dispatched to distant relatives in Alsace to be apprenticed with the Firm Carl Levy to learn the business of shopkeeping. The apprenticeship was cut short in 1916 by World War I, but not before Siegfried had become fluent in French.

Kenzingen was fiercely loyal to its German nationality and roused its young men to prove their patriotism by enlisting in the German army. By the end of 1916, Julius and Siegfried, good Germans both, had signed up. Julius served in the artillery. Siegfried, because of his knowledge of French, was assigned to the quartermaster corps. He spent the war years helping to requisition food and other supplies from the French countryside for the German army. When the war ended in 1918, soldiers were demobilized. Siegfried had hoped to continue his apprenticeship in Alsace, but the business had been liquidated during the war. Realizing how difficult it would be for him to earn a living in Kenzingen at that time, he decided to reenlist in the army as a civilian employee until September 1919, when he finally returned to civilian life, the proud bearer of his country's Iron Cross.

Back in Kenzingen, Siegfried spent the next year looking for work and helping his parents in the store. In November 1920, he found a position with Epstein and Co. in their office in the nearby city of Freiburg. He worked there for seven and a half years. By then, his father was ready to retire from active participation in the store, and Siegfried took over. The store was officially retitled Ludwig Dreifuss and Son.

Kenzingen soccer team, 1918. Siegfried is standing 5th from left

Siegfried's experiences over the past decade had stimulated his ambitions and broadened his horizons, so that he was eager to expand the shop beyond the confines of Kenzingen. By 1928, he had obtained a driver's license and became among the first in the village to own a car -- a green Opel, with some storage space in its rumble seat (an area

Outing to Switzerland with friends, 1927; Siegfried seated on left

in the rear of the car that opened outward to provide not only storage space, but also a seat for a passenger). With his new car, he was able to take merchandise from the shop out into the countryside, providing a useful service to the farmers who were scattered throughout the area and could not come to the village easily. This innovation proved good business for Ludwig Dreifuss and Son. Siegfried also became a popular and eligible bachelor about town. "Der Sigger" was welcome in homes everywhere in the village, for card games like Skat and pinochle or simply to visit. The villagers were proud of the man who owned a car and affectionately called the Opel "Der Sigger's *Gruene Kaefer*" (Siegfried's green bug). He became active in the village sports club as a valued member of the soccer team. In the winter, he bowled with a village team and enjoyed socializing in the local tavern after games. He sang in the village chorus, and went with his buddies on annual outings and hikes to various vacation areas. Pictures of the time show him as a dapper young man, notably not mustachioed like his friends, wearing his suits with considerable style, and well aware of his "better profile." Alas, by then he was already quite bald!

The Freiburg Connections: My Mother's Family

Freiburg im Breisgau was (and remains) a university city with a major cathedral and a long history and rich tradition. It saw itself as a cultural and intellectual center for the area, proud of its opera house and theaters. Much of its medieval architecture was maintained into the twentieth century (and rebuilt after World War II), including the city gates and main squares surrounded by medieval guild houses and the city hall. Among its signature features were the *baechle,* narrow, open canalettes, which were the city's open sewers in past times; they had been cleaned up by the nineteenth century when a modern sewer system was installed, but still maintained tiny rivulets of water coursing through them. They were, of course, irresistible attractions to the small children growing up in the city.

Freiburg was closed to Jews until 1863. Once permitted to become residents, the Jews quickly took advantage of the opportunities offered by the urban environment. Within half a decade, the sizable Jewish community had acquired its own cemetery and built a synagogue. The synagogue was centrally and conspicuously located next to the university on a slight rise of ground. It was built in a style quite traditional in the area, with an imposing entrance door, a large first floor prayer hall, with *bimah* (reader's desk) in the middle and the *aron kodesh* (ark containing the Torah) on the eastern wall. Surrounding the main hall, at the second level, was the women's gallery. The synagogue symbolized the security and prosperity of the Jewish community of Freiburg.

Over the next several decades, the Jewish community flourished and was able to provide its members not only with the necessary ritual facilities like synagogue, *mikveh*, and cemetery, but also kosher butcher shops, delicatessens, and bakeries. A small community center was built near the synagogue; it served as religious school and secondary prayer hall.

Freiburg became a magnet for Jews from small communities within at least a 50 mile radius. Among those attracted to Freiburg was Sigmund Valfer (my maternal grandfather), who had grown up in Gengenbach and later moved to Friesenheim. He was one of five surviving children of Jacob Hirsch Valfer. Jakob owned a wine store in Gengenbach, but did not expect Sigmund to succeed him. Sigmund was instead apprenticed as a house painter, paperhanger, and carpenter, but in Freiburg found other opportunities as a salesman for a variety of products. His bride, Anna Weil, grew up in Emmendingen. Like most children -- and as the law demanded -- she finished elementary school. She was then apprenticed to a dressmaker, and remained a fine seamstress into her adult years. Like her sister and two brothers (Betty, Ludwig, and Theo), she eventually moved to Freiburg.

Gretel with mother Anna Valfer, 1912

In 1906, Anna bore Sigmund a daughter, Grete (Gretel). Anna's labor was long and difficult, and Sigmund, seeing his young wife's pain, swore never to put her through such an ordeal again. And so, Gretel remained an only child. Among her closest playmates were two of her cousins -- Betty and Siegfried Mayer's daughter Ilse, and Ludwig and Margarethe's

Cousins Ilse Mayer, Gretel Valfer, and Hanna Weil, 1916

daughter Hanna. Bearing girls seems to have been a family tradition, since Theo and his wife Hilde also had daughters -- Lisa, Erna, and Toni. Gretel and Ilse were particularly close, probably because their mothers were very attached to each other and because the two families lived in the same apartment building in Karteuserstrasse, a quiet neighborhood of three story buildings just outside the old city walls.

The Valfers and Mayers seem to have been comfortably middle class. Sigmund Valfer for a time sold a variety of household products, including shoe polish, which he made in his own kitchen. But when the apartment almost burned down as a result of an accident while boiling the polish, he changed jobs and became a wine salesman, echoing the work of his father. The position apparently suited him, allowed him to travel, and enabled him to indulge his only daughter with occasional gifts – a jade and gold ring, a set of art deco inlaid wooden boxes, a folding ivory fan, which I still treasure. Gretel and Ilse went through secondary school together,

Fastnacht, 1928. Ilse Mayer and Gretel Valfer with friend

and, as they grew up, developed friendships with a number of the Jewish community's young intellectuals. They were both given piano lessons and learned a good bit of the dual piano literature.

Gretel was by far the quieter of the two. Ilse was known for her irrepressible spirits and love of fun. It was hard to keep her quiet or even to punish her. Once, when she lost track of time while "sailing boats" in Freiburg's *baechle*, her parents sought to teach her punctuality; they did so by locking her in the coal cellar for an hour. When they returned to fetch what they hoped would be a contrite Ilse, they found her contentedly playing "train" using the coal pieces as train cars! Even Gretel occasionally showed signs of rebellion at what was undoubtedly a constraining set of behaviors for good middle class German Jewish girls. When given a doll with the period's usual china head and told that it was not to be played with, but only displayed, she didn't hesitate to place it carefully by a door and then slam the door so that the doll's head was crushed!

During World War I, Gretel, like so many German children, was malnourished. She received supplementary milk rations, but they were apparently not enough to ensure healthy bone and teeth development. By her teens, Gretel had developed extreme buckteeth. Indicative of their comfortable circumstances, Anna and Sigmund agreed to have the teeth straightened. That required two years of braces, and Gretel went to the dentist every week to have the braces tightened. In the process she became most interested in dentistry and would have been happy to enter a dental school. But in the 1920s, that was quite a daring hope for a quiet young woman, and in 1923 Gretel instead was apprenticed as a secretary in the leather goods firm of P.J. Demuth Nachfolger. It was left to the more adventurous and younger Hanna to set her sights high and enroll in medical school, an education aborted by the rise of Nazism.

Gretel's apprenticeship apparently went extremely well. At the end of one year, her employer was so satisfied that he hired her to continue as bookkeeper/secretary in his office. Gretel stayed with the firm for two more years, at which time she opted to work for her uncles. When she left, her employer wrote her a glowing letter of recommendation. "Miss Grete Valfer was head cashier and performed exceptionally well, with great industriousness and honesty. She has carried out her obligations to my fullest satisfaction, so that I can recommend her most strongly. She is leaving my firm voluntarily. I wish her great success in her future endeavors."

I don't know why Gretel left what seems to have been a very satisfactory position to work for her uncles. I suspect that a good deal of pressure was put on her mother, Anna (Theo and Ludwig's sister), who was considered by the brothers to be something of a poorer relation. Anna probably felt that they could not refuse the offer, and Gretel obediently changed jobs.

On April 1, 1926, Gretel began to work for the *Gebrueder* Weil – her uncles Theo and Ludwig. She remained with them until her marriage in 1930. This was not an ideal situation. As a relative, she was often asked to do more than her position required and to work longer hours. Her pay was also not as generous as she had hoped. In any case, a salary at that time had little meaning because of the rampant inflation. Gretel remembered that on payday she took a small suitcase to work to hold her salary of many almost worthless deutschmarks. She then quickly went shopping, before they lost even more value. A week's wages often enabled her to buy nothing more than a set of underwear!

During her working years, Gretel continued to have an active social life. She and Ilse delighted in the annual *Fastnacht* (Mardi Gras)

Engagement party of Gretel Valfer and Siegfried Dreifuss (seated center), Freiburg, 1929

festivities, and often dressed in matching or complementary costumes emphasizing the shortness of Ilse and the relative height of Gretel. They obviously had a good time. Gretel also enjoyed informal classes at the university and continued playing the piano. She had a number of suitors, but for a variety of reasons ("His hands were so hairy," for example) she made no long-term attachments. Gretel commuted to work by trolley. Siegfried Dreifuss also often rode the trolley in his business activities around Freiburg, and he began to notice a vivacious young woman who seemed to ride the trolley on the same schedule. Curious about her, he asked a second cousin, Hanna Weil. Hanna knew Gretel very well, since they were first cousins. Hanna made the introductions, and this time Gretel found no faults. By late 1929, they were engaged. The wedding, conducted by the rabbi of the Freiburg synagogue, was held at the Valfer home on October 30, 1930. It was attended only by the closest relatives, including Siegfried's parents from Kenzingen. After the ceremony, they all joined in a celebratory dinner at a nearby restaurant.

Life in Kenzingen

Gretel had no hesitation about moving to Kenzingen once she and Siegfried were married. In preparation for the move, the third floor apartment of the Dreifuss family house on Brotstrasse was renovated. The two rooms across the front of the house became bedroom and living room. A set of wardrobes with art-deco veneer doors, and matching beds and night tables were installed in the bedroom. The night tables were essential since they doubled as commodes, and contained the potties for use during the night. The toilet was located at the far end of the apartment along an unheated exterior corridor. Among the furniture in the living room were bookcases, Gretel's piano, a large table and chairs, and a radio. In back of the living room, and extending to the covered back porch was the kitchen. The kitchen contained built-in cupboards and drawers, all painted white, and the latest in wood-burning stoves. In the center of the kitchen sat a table and chairs. On one side of the apartment, in back of the bedroom, but with no direct connection to it, was the parlor -- dark and full of heavy upholstered furniture and a sideboard containing "good" dishes and wedding gifts. The room was to be used only for entertaining visitors, though I have no memory of anyone ever being worthy of such an honor. It was aired and cleaned once a year, before *Pesach* (Passover). Across the entire back of the house and around one side was a covered porch. At its extreme end was a toilet/lavatory.

In its configuration, the apartment was very similar to that of Siegfried's parents, one floor below. But that apartment had never been modernized, so that its kitchen was quite dark and dominated by a floor-to-ceiling green tiled oven that served to heat the apartment. Cooking was done on burners over a wood fire, and anything that needed to be baked – such as *Berches* (challah) or *kugel* -- was brought to the bakery on the corner of the street. The kitchen was clearly the heart of that apartment.

It could not have been easy for Gretel to move to a small village from the sophistication and activities available in a large city like Freiburg. And living with one's in-laws must have been difficult as well, especially since Louis and Lina were quite conservative and traditional in their outlook, as was Bertha, Louis' unmarried sister who lived with them. Yet, Gretel always maintained that she was never homesick nor had she any regrets about the change in her lifestyle. She always affirmed that the love she and Siegfried had for each other overrode any negatives.

The young couple was welcomed into Kenzingen's social life. Siegfried continued his sports activities. He still sang in the village glee club and played cards regularly with his buddies. Gretel made friends with many of the village women and joined in *kaffee klatsches.* They participated fully in village festivities, like *Fastnacht* (Mardi Gras) and the *Weinachtsmarkt* (Christmas market). For *Fastnacht*, Gretel loved elaborate costumes and delighted in disguises that made her unrecognizable to Siegfried. One year she dressed as a harem slave, complete with pale green veil and ivory slave bracelet. Siegfried had no idea who was wearing that costume and flirted with her all evening! The Weinachtsmarkt in early December, conveniently located just in back of the Dreifuss house on the church square, was a fine opportunity for Siegfried to set up a stall along with those from other shops in the village and sell fabrics and household goods to farmers from the entire region. By the early 1930s, the household goods store of Dreifuss and Sons was well known in the region, and was thriving.

Siegfried had by then virtually taken over the business, leaving Louis with little to do. He filled in his time by becoming a tobacco jobber. He bought the freshly harvested tobacco leaves from the farmers in the area and used the loft over the garage at the rear of the courtyard for tobacco curing. He would then resell the dried leaves to agents who, in turn, sold the cured tobacco to the region's cigar factories. This was clearly a small operation, but it provided Louis with his own activity and bit of income.

Despite their integration into village life, the Dreifusses remained observant Jews. Shabbat was honored: The store was closed, and the family spent the day quietly at home, or taking long walks into the countryside, or simply sitting in front of their house. Years later, a peasant neighbor remembered that he was always a little jealous that the Jews had a day completely free of chores and hoped that in some future life, he, too, might be born a Jew! Since none of the family was able to turn on lights or stoke the ovens, a *schabbes goy* (non-Jewish assistant for Shabbat) was pressed into service. He would come on Friday and Saturday afternoons, when dark came early in the day, and light the special *schabbes* lamps that hung in the kitchens of the two apartments. Made of brass, with six arms extending in a circle from the central core, they burned oil wicks and provided just enough light to allow activities to continue. The *schabbes goy* was often a young boy, who was paid in chocolate nonpareils for his help.

Of course, the young couple kept kosher. Since Kenzingen had no kosher butcher, meat and cold cuts of all kinds were obtained in nearby Emmendingen or Eichstetten, or in Freiburg when they visited there. Occasionally, a *schochet* (ritual slaughterer) would come through Kenzingen, and provide a few chickens freshly slaughtered. In the days before Pesach, the goose that my grandmother Lina had raised in the small courtyard and that she had been force-feeding with careful regularity would fall to the knife. Whenever fresh poultry became available in this way, the ritual of cleaning the birds fell to Lina. A great pot of steaming water was brought out to facilitate plucking feathers, though care was taken not to immerse the bird itself in the water, lest the blood coagulate and, thereby, make it unkosher. Cleaning the insides of the bird was an activity I watched in great fascination. Lina was always especially careful when pulling out the liver, lest the gall bladder, with its bile, rupture and make the liver too bitter to use. It was all a great lesson in bird anatomy. For our kosher household, in the days before vegetable shortenings, chickens and geese were essential sources of fat that could be used for making meat meals. The skin was rendered and provided not just fat, but also crispy *griebe* (cracklings).

The diet generally was a mix of local foods and traditionally Jewish foods, which, for us, meant many of the traditions of Alsace, where the family had originated. Potatoes were a staple, served in many guises. Vegetables were fresh only during the summer; for the remainder of the year, we relied on the supply that Lina had preserved. Bread was generally a heavy rye or pumpernickel. White rolls were a special treat, especially for youngsters, distributed by village families on very special occasions like weddings. Among the local dishes, suet *kugel* (pudding) was a favorite. This dish, sure to clog any arteries, was somewhat the equivalent of the East European *cholent* (a meat and vegetable/bean dish usually cooked overnight in a very slow oven), since it was baked in stages and could be kept hot in the oven for Shabbat. The suet for this dish often came from the brisket that was turned into sauerbraten. When topped with stewed prunes or pears, *kugel* was a winter treat. Organ meats were widely used, especially tongue and lungs, cooked sweet and sour style. For dairy meals, *spaetzle* (homemade noodles) were served layered with freshly cooked green beans and generously topped with melted butter and croutons. The influence of Alsace made itself known in the mix of sauerkraut and mashed potatoes, served hot and accompanied by sausages. Sausage also was a key ingredient in potato soup. A dessert favorite, chestnuts cooked with prunes, also has Alsatian antecedents. A pastry with strong Kenzingen roots was *linzertorte.* This delicious tart was made of nut-based dough, topped with raspberry jam. Lina always made two at a time and, since it kept well for a very long time, reserved one for guests or to bring to post-funeral meals.

Mama enjoyed cooking and brought with her to Kenzingen some of the more sophisticated dishes of city life. In the summer, when fresh peaches were available, she made an elegant dessert – *Goetterspeise* (food of the gods), which layered sponge cake, peaches, and wine cream. She baked a variety of cookies, including the German Christmas favorite, *Lebkuchen.* Even everyday foods were often given a special twist. Devilled eggs were decorated with parsley or paprika; pudding was set into individual molds. This especially impressed some of the village children who remembered, even into old age, that, whereas their mothers simply spooned out pudding from a big bowl, Frau Dreifuss served it in beautiful individual shapes!

Going to synagogue services was seldom an option, since the nearest synagogue was in Emmendingen. Some Dreifuss cousins lived there, and provided a place to stay when Louis and Lina went to High Holy Day services. Siegfried and Gretel drove to Freiburg to stay with Gretel's parents for holidays throughout the year so that they could attend services in the Freiburg synagogue.

The major holiday celebrated by the family in Kenzingen itself was Pesach (Passover), which occasioned the gathering in the family home of all the brothers and their wives for the *seders*. Weeks of work went into preparation, as Lina scrubbed and scoured every conceivable pot and dish, including the glass jars kept in the attic for preserving fruits and vegetables. Everything was dragged into the corridor off the kitchen, where a great pot of steaming water was kept for the clean-up. All the rooms were also turned inside out, feather beds and rugs were aired, and the parlors in both apartments were opened for their annual breath of fresh air.

Once all was satisfactorily cleaned, the special Pesach dishes were brought out and the cleaning began all over again with them. These dishes included great bowls and pots, since it was the one time of the year when a large number of people were fed. Julius, my father's older brother, arrived with his wife Meta. They lived in Duesseldorf, where Julius was employed by an optical firm. Younger brother Max, also in opticals, arrived from Berlin with his wife, Gretel. Neither Meta nor Gretel had been born Jewish, but both immersed themselves into Judaism and fully participated in the family celebrations. Adolf, the youngest of the brothers and unmarried, attended as often as he could.

The *seder* itself was conducted by my grandfather Louis. He used a round silver *seder* plate with three tiers, for the three *matzot* that are a part of the *seder* ritual. The meal included both small *matzoh* balls in the chicken soup, and larger *matzoh* dumplings that accompanied the main course, the highlight of which was the goose that Lina had raised all year. The force-feeding not only provided a plump bird, but also the enlarged liver (foie gras) and the fatty skin for rendering into goose fat and *griebe*. After all, what could be better than a *matzoh* with a layer of fatty, crisp skin and onions! Once the meal was finished, Lina repaired to the kitchen to tackle the dishes. But she couldn't resist reappearing back at the *seder*, a bowl and dishtowel tucked under her arm, to join along with everyone else as the concluding songs were sung. As the final number, the family had a unique ditty –*Yockele will Birne pflikke"* –a Baden version of *Had Gad Yah* (a song about buying a goat), about a young girl who was sent out to pick pears and suffered a sequence of misfortunes.

By the spring of 1931, Gretel was pregnant. Great excitement in the Dreifuss family, since none of the other sons seemed to be producing offspring. Gretel felt well, and indulged herself in the fresh fruits and vegetables that were so abundant in the countryside. She picked great handfuls of cherries in the nearby orchards and delighted in the baskets of tomatoes that friends brought to her. The hospital in Kenzingen was run by the nuns of the town's cloister, and Siegfried and Gretel made arrangements for the birth to occur there. On September 25, I made my appearance under the gentle care of the nun-midwives. Being a girl, I was apparently carrying on the line of girls in my mother's family, but, to the delight of the Dreifuss side, the all-boys pattern was finally broken. The nuns were particularly solicitous of my mother's dietary needs as an observant Jew and assured her that the *Wienerschnitzel* (veal cutlets) they were serving had been cooked only in butter! Mama ate the food that her family brought.

Alice, Kenzingen, 1932

I was named after Auguste, an aunt of Papa's, the late sister of my grandfather. But Mama insisted that no child of hers would carry such a name. So the compromise was reached of retaining the Hebrew name, *Gitel*, but using the secular name Alice. The name was made official a few weeks after my birth at a *Hollegrasch*. The origins of this ceremony are obscure, though some speculate that it derives from an old French custom of raising the cradle (*haute la crèche*) at the time a girl is named. At any rate, the occasion called for a gathering of the family, including the Freiburger Oma and Opa (grandparents), and of all the friends in town, especially the children. In keeping with tradition, the children present gathered around the cradle and lifted it three times, chanting, "*Hollegrasch,* what will the child's name be?" The children were then given keepsakes of the occasion – bags made of beautiful marbelized papers, filled with all kinds of sweets. The surplus bags were stored in a kitchen drawer, and, once I was old enough, I delighted in pulling them out and hearing the story of how I was named.

As the first grandchild on either side of the family, I was showered with love and attention. Aunt Meta, who was an accomplished seamstress, sewed smocked silk dresses for me; Oma and Opa in Freiburg provided me with stuffed animals. In Kenzingen, I had more than enough doting relatives to look after me. It must have been an enormous challenge for my parents to keep me from getting utterly spoiled. But in good German tradition, they were very particular about schedules and behavior in general, and I was kept to strict standards.

In the small apartment in which we lived, there was no separate room for a child. My crib, and eventually, my bed were simply placed across the foot of my parents' bed, and room was made in the wardrobes for my clothing. In time, the potty in the nightstand became my toilet for training. I continued to use it as a young child and happily scooted on it around the perimeter of the big bed, braiding the fringes on the bedcover, while doing my "duty." I liked it much better than the "big" toilet at the far end of the house.

The next two years were happy and relaxed. Business prospered, and the young Dreifuss couple was confidently looking forward to a comfortable life. They continued their involvement in Kenzingen, with the added pleasure of sharing childcare with willing grandparents who enabled Mama and Papa to take excursions to favorite vacation spots, like Bodensee, Titisee, or sites in Switzerland. Neighborhood children flocked to our home and, as soon as I was old enough, some of

Alice as Little Red Riding Hood, Fastnacht in Kenzingen, 1933

the village youngsters were delighted to take me for walks in the pram or to play with me at home. The most memorable escapade on these outings occurred in the spring when I was about two years old. While on a walk, we wandered down to the River Els, which runs through the village. I came a bit too close to the banks and tumbled in. My friends quickly pulled me out, but I had ruined a brand new white coat that I was wearing for the first time. The story of my rescue became part of village lore, remembered well into the future.

Trips to Freiburg, made easy because of Papa's Opel, were occasions for showing me off to relatives – at the time, I was the only child born to any of the Weil cousins – and letting my Oma and Opa there help take care of me. Mama and Papa took advantage of their help to continue attending cultural events, including the annual New Year's Eve opera (*Die Fledermaus*) and ball held on the opera house stage. We also took advantage of Freiburg's superior medical services to go there for dental and medical visits. Our dentist, Isi Picard, tried very hard to make these visits pleasant for me and rewarded me with honey cake. But since I disliked honey cake, the bribe didn't work, and I continued resisting dental care.

Memories of the early years in Kenzingen include many hours spent with my Opa and Oma there. I loved watching Oma cook, especially when she made *Schopfnudeln*, potato-based noodles that are rolled out as long as possible. I delighted in helping to roll them. I often followed her down to the root cellar – a cool, dank basement with a packed dirt floor, where large bins of potatoes and huge barrels of sauerkraut were stored. Each fall, these stores were replenished when an itinerant sauerkraut maker came by and shredded mounds of cabbages for pickling. Jars of fruit and vegetables that she had preserved herself were also stored in the cellar, as was wine.

In the quiet hours of Shabbat afternoon, I often sat in my Opa's lap, to be treated to a chocolate bar and tickled by his mustache. This wasn't always pleasant, since he used snuff that had a rather strong odor and turned his white mustache mustard yellow. As soon as I was old enough, he took me for walks, and I delighted in walking a bit behind him so I could tickle the hands he clasped behind his back. I generally loved to tease him, for he always took it in good humor, and would retaliate by carefully placing my dolls upside down, which he knew would upset me greatly. During thunderstorms, I turned to him, because I knew he would hold me in his arms and show me how thunder and lightning were really beautiful and not frightening

Not all my memories of those early years are positive. I was terrified of the chimney sweep, whose thin, all-black presence – black hat, black suit and shoes, and black face and hands – appeared annually. I dove under the kitchen table and stayed there until he was gone, despite all the assurances that Mama could give. And then there was the adventure with Papa's wedding ring when I was about four. Papa often left his ring on the nightstand next to his bed when he went out to cut wood for the kitchen stove. Since my crib and, eventually, bed had been placed across the foot of my parents' bed, I saw the ring regularly when I took my nap. One afternoon, I decided to play with it by flipping it against my lower lip. Suddenly, it flew out of my fingers and into my throat. My parents tried to have me cough it up, but when that failed to produce the ring, they took me to the local doctor. He was certain that, given time, it would show up in my stool. Two days passed, with still no sign of the ring. And I was beginning to have difficulty swallowing and breathing. An x-ray showed that the ring had become lodged in my throat and was surrounded by mucus. My parents rushed me to the hospital in Freiburg, where doctors were able to pull it out. I was pleased to be able to spend a night in the hospital, with Mama alongside. The most memorable event of the stay was being served soup in a cup (how odd not to use a plate or bowl) and blowing it very hard to cool it off!

The routine of the Jewish calendar and holidays became a normal part of my life. For Rosh Hashanah, we traveled to Freiburg to attend the synagogue with my Freiburg grandparents. I always knew this was a very special holiday, since Mama wore her best dress and Papa was resplendent in his *zylinder* – a collapsible black silk opera hat. Although the synagogue service was considered modern - the sermon was preached in German, it nonetheless followed the Orthodox tradition of separate seating for men and women. My Oma, Mama, and I sat in the upper gallery, while the men sat on the main floor. But the seating was carefully arranged, so that my Opa and Papa sat on one side of the floor and we womenfolk sat in the gallery on the opposite side. That way we could signal to each other in simple hand and eye communication. I loved sitting next to my Oma, since she always wore her best black silk dress in honor of the occasion and a tiny black hat with a veil pulled tightly over her face; she carried a tiny beaded black purse that contained a handkerchief scented with "4711 Eau de Cologne." For jewelry she wore a gold watch on a long gold chain, which I delighted in listening to – it had a strong tick-tock – and opening to look at the delicate dial. In fact, I considered this to be "my" watch, and regularly checked on it in its drawer whenever we visited Freiburg.

We returned to Freiburg for Yom Kippur. Oma always considered this her favorite holiday, since it was the only time of the year when she had absolutely no duties at home. For Yom Kippur, Opa left the more modern atmosphere of the big synagogue to attend the even more traditional services being held in the small community center next door. Each year, once I was old enough, he took me with him to listen to the *shofar* (a ram's horn used in religious services), and since I was a child,

I was able to stay with him among all the assembled men. All were dressed in their white *sargeness* (a linen garment designed to serve as a shroud upon death, and usually presented to the groom by his bride on their wedding), with great *tallesim* (prayer shawls) thrown over their heads. My Opa took me under his *tallit* to hear the *shofar*, carefully instructing me never to look at the *shofar* as it was being blown. To this day, I have never actually seen the blowing of the *shofar* during the service, and my grandfather is always at my side for the occasion.

Family gathering in Kenzingen, 1934. From left: Max and Gretel Dreifuss, Oma, Alice, Opa, Aunt Bertha, Mama, Papa

Sukkot was celebrated in both Kenzingen and Freiburg. At home, we celebrated with freshly baked *berches (challah,* braided bread*),* newly pressed cider, and freshly picked walnuts. In Freiburg, we went *sukkah* (a temporary hut) hopping. Although my grandparents, who lived in an apartment in center city, weren't able to put up a *sukkah,* many of their friends did. I especially loved the one that Rabbi Picard had. The Picards were good friends and distant relatives (their son, Isi, was our dentist) and we were always welcome to visit. Their *sukkah* was made of wood and the interior was completely covered with painted scenes of country life. Built into one wall was a small compartment, opened with a spring, in which a small *Torah* was stored. The fir boughs that covered the roof were decorated with grapes and walnuts covered in tin foil. We usually visited Freiburg toward the end of *Sukkot*, so that we were able to stay and celebrated *Simchat Torah* (Rejoicing in the Law) as well. I loved to parade in the synagogue with the other children and get showered with candies from the ladies sitting in the gallery. Eventually, Opa made me a flag to carry – half white, half light blue, with a gold Star of David in the center – that was more beautiful than any that the other children had.

Chanukah was such a minor holiday that I have no special memory of it at all. Purim was marked in Kenzingen only within the family. We read the *megillah* (scroll of Esther), but more important, Oma made *Purimkichle.* These pastries were made of sweet yeast dough with raisins, chunks of which were pulled into triangular shapes and then deep-fat fried and sprinkled with sugar and cinnamon. Mama made her own version – also of a sweet yeast dough, but hers were more like jelly doughnuts.

For the first three years of their marriage, Mama and Papa seemed to have everything going well for them. A flourishing business, a healthy child, satisfying social activities, and strong support from parents all provided a happy life. In 1933, Hitler came to power. Life began to unravel, slowly at first, then with increasing speed and menace. The happy, contented expressions in the early pictures of the young couple were replaced by the haunted look of hunted people.

Chased Like a Mongrel Dog

In 1933, Hitler came to power; the pleasant, comfortable life of our family in Kenzingen, like that of Jews everywhere in Germany, was eroded. We had the misfortune of living in an area of Germany that was especially nationalistic. As the transit route for armies from many nations in many wars, the burgers of Baden were eager to prove that they were good Germans all, ready and willing to carry out their Fuehrer's decrees. Regulations that may have been applied only half-heartedly in other areas of Germany were enforced quickly and thoroughly in our little corner. And so, the happiness that shone from Mama's face as she looked at her tiny family was replaced by the look of a terrified woman. The future and the financial success of the family that seemed so sure shuddered to a stop. Friends melted away, activities were curtailed, money became scarce, and even the food on the table underwent transformations. The tragedy that struck all Jews living in Germany in the Nazi years was felt early in the southwest.

The first direct change in Kenzingen came when Papa was informed that he could no longer be a member of the village *Sportverein* (Sports Club) and was no longer welcome to be on its soccer team. "Der Sigger" was a good soccer player and a long-time member of the club; but Hitler decreed that Jews were poor sportsmen and therefore a pollutant on Aryan sports teams, sure to destroy any chance of success. So Siegfried was expelled. Some members of the team undoubtedly felt they were loosing a good player, but no one spoke out against the action. The law was the law, and, as good Germans, the club members obeyed. Papa didn't raise objections because he saw the law as absurd and sure to be rescinded. Hitler appeared to many as an aberration that simply had to be put up with until he was replaced. No point in making a fuss. German Jews for many decades had become expert at not making a fuss, at practicing their religion at home, but being secular in public and thus seeming to integrate into general German society.

The decree against Jews in sports extended to bowling as well. So Papa had to resign from his bowling club and give up the weekly winter evenings of bowling, followed by beer with friends at a local *Bierstube* (pub). The culmination of these minor exclusions came one evening when the Kenzingen Glee Club, in which Papa sang regularly, finished their concert by singing *Deutschland Ueber Alles* (the German national anthem) and raising their arms in the Hitler salute. Papa refused to sing or salute and was chased out of the room "like a mongrel dog." One of the singers remembered years afterward, "We all knew that this wasn't right, but we let it go and didn't say anything." Their pride of nationalism trumped their conscience. The exclusion of the Jews had begun by making them marginal in many social and civic activities. As a first step in achieving a Germany that was *Judenrein* (clean of Jews), Hitler's far reach succeeded in making Jews unwelcome in the very circles where they had felt so comfortable in the past.

Alice in Kenzingen, 1936

I felt little of these early changes. My friends continued to flock to my house, attracted by my many toys. Little girls delighted in playing with my doll collection. Few had store-bought dolls with expressive faces and wardrobes of clothes; theirs were more likely to be homemade rag dolls. Similarly, my rocking horse, kept on the large back porch, was far more attractive than the makeshift brooms with rag tails that most children had. My toy kitchen, complete with pots and pans and a small tea service, was a magnet for boys and girls. Papa even made me a child-sized market stall, like the one he had for the Christmas market, which was outfitted with tiny bolts of cloth and had built-in drawers for coins. I may have been the only Jewish child in Kenzingen, but for the first four years of my life, I never lacked playmates.

Then, in 1935, over a period of several months, Hitler promulgated the Nuremberg Laws. Jews were stripped of their citizenship, and the social marginalization that had begun in 1933 was augmented by strict economic curtailments that fell especially heavily on professionals and civil servants. A boycott of Jewish stores spread the hardships to businessmen like Papa as well. Jews were forbidden to buy goods from non-Jewish wholesalers, and Aryans were ordered not to patronize Jewish stores. At the same time, Jews were restricted in where and when they could shop; many establishments made it clear that Jews were not welcome on their premises. *Juden Verboten* (Jews prohibited) became a common sign scrawled on shop windows. To enforce the boycott, the Nazis resorted to pressure not only on Jews but also on Aryans. In Kenzingen, they posted men a few houses down on either side of our shop to take photos and record the names of anyone brave enough to enter the shop to make a purchase. These courageous villagers were subsequently visited and warned about never daring to break the boycott in the future. Most were duly intimidated. Customers vanished, although several brave neighbors, emboldened by the example of the parish priest, continued to buy from Papa, coming to the back door at night to avoid being spotted by the Nazi spies. Business in our store declined precipitously. Its inventory had been valued at about 50,000 mark (2.5 mark equaled $1) in 1932; by 1938, that value had fallen to only 2,000 mark. Lost income over the period was some 30,000 mark.

As a small child, I finally felt the impact of Nazi hatred as well. One of my big treats each summer, when we visited my grandparents in Freiburg, had been to go with my Oma to a café for ice cream. Served in a metal dish with two wafers, ice cream was available only in summer

Alice with Uncle Siegfried, Freiburg, 1938

and only in cafes. In the summer of 1936, we went for our treat as always, but found a huge *Juden Verboten* sign on the café's window. We dared not enter lest someone identify us as Jews and throw us out bodily. I never had ice cream in Germany again. Similarly, during that summer in Freiburg, on a walk with my Opa up the Hochberg, we stopped as usual at an inn along the trail to get some water from a fountain in the inn's courtyard. I looked forward to this, because Opa always brought along a collapsible cup and a packet of orangeade. But on this particular walk, I couldn't get my drink because a sign on the fountain proclaimed *Juden Verboten.* End of walks.

Also end of friends. As the Nazi propaganda intensified, people became afraid to be seen with Jews. Our village neighbors crossed the street when we appeared outdoors and kept their children away from our home. Only the Englers, who lived directly across the street from us, maintained their friendship. Even as a five-year old, I learned to avoid the ostracism of others by staying indoors.

Over the course of 1936 and 1937, our family struggled to keep a normal home and somehow provide enough income for our needs. Mama and Papa decided two things: One, they were not going to bring any more children into a world dominated by Hitler. This allowed them to sell all the baby furniture, clothing, and equipment that had been saved from my birth, and thereby augment the slight income from the shop. Our Christian neighbors were happy to buy these goods at well below market price. Two, they would try to leave Germany as soon as possible. The model for emigration was Mama's cousin, Ilse, who left for New York in 1936. On her way by train from Freiburg to the coast, she passed through Kenzingen, and Mama went to the railroad station for a last wave farewell. The train didn't stop, but Ilse had time to throw Mama a bouquet of red roses and a small farewell note. That bouquet, even once the flowers dried, was a treasured memento in our home and a spur for my parents to follow Ilse.

The effects of the Nazi laws were, of course, felt by my grandparents in Freiburg as well. My Opa there, who had been a wine salesman, lost his position. Fortunately, he had other skills to fall back on. Trained as a carpenter and painter, he began a new career. Some Jews were able to flee Germany, but they were prohibited from taking valuables with them. They devised ways to smuggle their jewelry and silver out of the country in a variety of ways, and my Opa helped by installing hollow arms and legs in their furniture. He thus was able earn some income quite steadily.

Much of the smuggling went through Switzerland, where many of the Jews in our region had relatives. That border remained quite accessible for a number of years and became the transit point for regular movement back and forth of people and goods. One of the many regulars was Rabbi Jakob Picard, who made it his mission to get as many religious objects out of Germany as possible. A diminutive man with a white beard, he became a familiar sight to the border guards. Once, while carrying a *shofar* across the border, he was stopped by suspicious guards, who demanded to know what he was carrying. Picard knew that the *shofar*, as a religious object, would be confiscated. He answered the guards by pretending to be hard of hearing; "What did you say?" he asked, cupping his ear with his hand. When they repeated the question, louder, he raised the *shofar* to his ear, like a hearing aid, "What did you say?" The guards gave up, laughingly recognizing that they'd never outsmart Picard, and let him through.

Among the Nazi edicts was a decree barring Jewish children from participating in public schools. At most, they were allowed to sit at the rear of the classroom, but were not to participate in any class discussions or activities. Instead, Jewish communities were ordered to organize their own schools, exclusively for Jewish children. This was obviously not a viable option in the many small villages and towns in our region, since most included only a few Jewish children. The Freiburg Jewish community, however, had enough children to organize a school for them. In 1935, they found a public facility – the Lessing Schule – that was willing to provide two rooms within its building for the Jewish school, rooms that had a separate side entrance so that the Jewish children could be kept totally isolated from their Aryan peers. The school also restricted the Jewish children's use of the playground to the few minutes when the Aryan children were not outdoors. This school served as a magnet for most of the Jewish children in nearby small communities. Some commuted daily, others boarded with relatives or friends, or became paying boarders in Freiburg's Jewish homes. Finding teachers was no problem, since Jewish teachers had all lost their positions in public schools and universities and were happy to have other employment.

The Jewish school tried to make life as normal as possible for its pupils. As long as possible under Nazi regulations, classes went on outings, held sporting events away from the school playground, and tried to cover a normal curriculum. But an important part of daily lessons were classes in English and Hebrew, in the hope that one or the other of these two languages would prove useful if/when the children were able to emigrate.

My parents were very reluctant to send me away from home when I first became old enough to go to school, and they certainly didn't want to expose me to possible harassment in Kenzingen's public school, where I would have been relegated to a silent role in the back row. So I was kept at home until the spring of 1938, when I moved in with my Oma and Opa in Freiburg and enrolled in the Jewish School. I was thrilled to be going to school and especially looked forward to the first day. To make learning sweet, I received a traditional large paper cone filled with cakes and candies. I was also very proud of my brand new *Mappe* (a small backpack) in which I kept new school books, notebooks, and a slate.

I was happy to spend time with my grandparents, since my Oma treated me very much the way my Mama did. Each night she read to me from one of the few children's books then available. A favorite was the novel, *Heimatlos* ("Nobody's Boy") by Hector Mallot, which always elicited great suspense and copious tears, even after the third or fourth reading. She often spoiled me with chocolate milk, since I refused to drink plain milk that had been boiled so that it formed a skin on top, though I always knew when she tried to fool me into drinking the cheaper Ovaltine instead. I loved to play with the long strips of paper that were left over from the rolls of lace and seam binding she used in sewing her dresses. I realize now that many of these activities were designed to fill the void of having no playmates and to keep me off the street, especially after I had been chased indoors one summer as "a Jewish pig that doesn't belong on the public street."

Since my grandparents lived in the center of the city at that time, my Oma escorted me to school daily, along the city's main street and over the bridge to the Lessing Schule. She also carefully picked me up at the end of the day. Like the other Jewish children, I was protected as much as possible from exposure to the Nazis. It was thus impossible to develop friendships with the other students in the Jewish School, since they, too were hustled in and out. We were all also reluctant to make new friends because our old ones had proved very fickle and deserted us when Jews became stigmatized. Still, I liked school and especially enjoyed the short recesses, when we could play with the chestnuts that had fallen off the trees surrounding the school. I remember very little about the class work, except that I thought English spelling absurd. Imagine spelling "here" when I knew it should be spelled "hier."

As part of the community's attempt to keep its Jewish children protected but also entertained and educated in Jewish matters, we had a kind of club at the small Jewish community center building next to the synagogue. We met on Shabbat afternoons, and played a variety of games designed to teach us some Hebrew vocabulary and also raise our awareness of Palestine. The game I remember best was called "Going to Jerusalem," which was simply musical chairs with a Jewish name. I think it reflected what our teachers wished for us.

In July 1938, when school recessed, as the public schools did, for a four-week summer vacation, I went home to Kenzingen, and then returned to school in August. I had no hesitation going back to Freiburg to live with my Oma and Opa again. My parents joined us for the High Holy Days, and we were able to celebrate *Sukkoth* and *Simchas Torah* in near normal fashion. I delighted in marching around the synagogue with the beautiful flag that my Opa had made for me. The synagogues during this difficult, uncertain time were often filled to overflowing as Jews sought comfort and community. School continued through the fall, and so I was not in Kenzingen on November 8 – Kristallnacht.

Kristallnacht – the night of broken glass and burning synagogues. Jewish school was abruptly cancelled, the beautiful Freiburger synagogue went up in flames, and the next day my Opa disappeared from our household. I have very few recollections of that horrible time, and was spared some of the worst sights because I was sheltered in my grandparents' apartment. But in a few days, my Mama came to take me home to Kenzingen, where the store was boarded up, and both my Papa and Opa were missing. Only decades later did I learn the story of Kristallnacht in Kenzingen.

All during the day of November 8, school children were mobilized to march in the village streets singing nationalistic and anti-semitic songs. Red flags with the black swastika hung from every possible window. Tension rose with each turn of the marching children and Hitler Youth through the streets. That evening, a group of men, ostensibly from the surrounding area, were organized by the Gestapo, plied with liquor, and marched into Kenzingen. There, they zeroed in on the only Jewish-owned shop in town -- ours, broke the glass window, and looted the store. The pitifully few goods remaining in the store were piled in a heap in the street. The men then went up to the third floor – my parents' home – and gathered all the books and piano sheet music they could find. These, too, they piled in a heap on top of the merchandise. And then they set fire to the entire mound, and kept the flames going through much of the night, while my terrorized parents and grandparents huddled helplessly in their home.

The next day, the Gestapo arrived in Kenzingen in open lorries. They went to each of the three houses in Kenzingen where Jews lived and arrested all the males age 16 and over. At the time, my Opa was out of the house, taking his usual morning walk in the countryside. Farmers told him that the police were looking for him, so, not wishing to get the family in more trouble, he hurried back home. He arrived just in time to take off his walking shoes and change into slippers before the Gestapo arrived. He and my Papa, like Jews all over southwestern Germany, were transported to the Dachau Concentration Camp. Many, like my relatives, were taken in open trucks, in plain sight of their neighbors. None in Kenzingen tried to stop the trucks or protest the deportations.

The truck went from village to village, collecting its victims, until the truck was full over capacity. Then it drove to a railroad station for the final journey to Dachau. On the way, the Gestapo did all they could to demean and dehumanize their human cargo. For example, the men were deprived of their belts and had their pants tied around their legs. They were then forced to drink castor oil -- a purgative -- to empty their bowels, with no possibility of using a toilet or cleaning up. After all, the Gestapo considered them all *Sheissjuden* (Jewish shit). My father's comment, typical of his dry, ironic sense of humor, was that this was done so that the Jews would smell just like the Gestapo! As soon as the prisoners arrived in Dachau, their heads were shaved and they were issued prison uniforms. They were also issued yellow stars, made of cloth, with *Jude* (Jew) imprinted on them. These they had to sew onto metal plates cut into six-pointed stars. They had to wear these at all times to distinguish them from the political prisoners already in the camp.

With the arrests of thousands of Jewish men all over Germany, the Nazis were faced with a totally inadequate system of concentration camps. Dachau had been set up early in the Nazi regime in an old ammunitions factory. It was soon rebuilt and designed to hold some 5,000 prisoners. It was immediately full with persons the Nazis deemed undesirable and a threat to the purity of the Aryan race. By 1937, some 13,260 inmates were held captive there. Dachau became the model for other concentration camps and a training ground for camp staff. Here, the yellow star was introduced to distinguish Jews from other prisoners held there in "protective custody."

The addition of some 11,000 Jews strained the abominable situation in Dachau even further, with not enough space to house the prisoners, very little food, and almost no medical help. To relieve the pressure, the Nazis decided that Jewish men, especially those age 50 and over, would be released from the camp if they (or their families) could prove that they were about to emigrate from Germany. After all, the aim of the Nazis was to make Germany *Judenrein*, and the deportation of the Jewish men was designed to frighten them enough to want to leave as quickly as possible. As if Germany's Jews were not already terrified!

The day after the deportations, Gretel (Mama) was delegated by our family to go to Emmendingen, just a few kilometers from Kenzingen, to check on the various family members who lived there. As she made her way along the streets, the glass of the many shattered store windows crunched under foot. Destruction had been thorough: stores had been vandalized and the synagogue burned to the ground. The stones in the old Jewish cemetery had been overturned and many were smashed. A teacher in the school overlooking the burial ground watched and commented to his students, "You'll see, eventually, you'll pay for each stone that's destroyed." Like Kenzingen, Emmendingen had been stripped of its Jewish men, including several of the Dreifuss cousins like Emil, who had been a successful attorney in the town.

Once she was back home, Mama made arrangements to bring me home from Freiburg. And she organized the paperwork related to the family's efforts to emigrate to the United States. She cabled the US Consulate in Stuttgart to beg for a speedy response – and waited in vain for a reply. Nonetheless, with the help of the Kenzingen parish priest, she took the documents she had on hand to the local Gestapo as proof that we were trying to leave Germany. As a result of her efforts, Papa and both my grandfathers were released from Dachau on December 6, just a month after being deported.

My memory of that traumatic time is very scant, although I do remember coming back to a home without Papa. I also remember quite vividly Papa's return home, with not even the fringe of hair that he usually sported around his bald head, and with a very terrible, sad expression in his eyes. He never spoke to me about those dreadful days. I learned only indirectly of the many humiliations that the men had to endure, of the long hours standing at attention on the parade ground while one of their fellows was drowned in three inches of water or hanged from the ever-present gallows. Always, I learned, Papa's sense of humor remained intact and helped keep up the morale of those near him. In addition to his secret memories, Papa brought home with him one souvenir – the yellow star that he always called his "graduation certificate" from Dachau.

No Place to Raise a Child

As life became increasingly difficult in Kenzingen, as it did for Jews everywhere in Germany, my parents began to think seriously about leaving. The image of Ilse on the train to Hamburg, the bouquet of roses she had tossed Mama, and the mail we received from her since her arrival in New York were powerful prods to emigrate to America. Ilse's experience seemed so positive. She had been able to obtain a post as a children's nanny for a very wealthy, well-placed family in New York, even though she had had little use for small children, including me. She seemed content with the position, liked the family, and made friends with other young women in similar positions. Summers were spent with her employer family at beaches in New Jersey, and vacations in nearby mountain resorts.

So the United States seemed to us like a logical choice. The possibility was reinforced by a stream of news clippings that Ilse sent to keep us informed about life in America, which was not always positive, as the stories about the 1938 hurricane indicated; she also sent me books starring Shirley Temple that I adored having, even though I couldn't read a word in them. But seeing a cute, curly haired young girl in dreamy, fantasy stories made America seem like a very wonderful place to me.

But there were powerful reasons to remain in Kenzingen, not the least of which were two sets of elderly parents who were terrified at the thought of going to a foreign country, where they neither knew the language nor had friends. Besides, they were so sure that Hitler was just a passing phenomenon, and that the madness would soon be over and order restored. And leaving Germany and getting into the United States was no easy task. Germany had to issue passports, which involved a complex process in which the applicants had to prove that no taxes were owed and that they had no criminal record. The Nuremberg Laws provided a further complication since they deprived Jews of their German citizenship, making it difficult for Jews to obtain passports if they didn't already have them. We had also heard how very difficult it was to obtain the proper documents to be admitted into the Untied States. Throughout 1937, Mama and Papa thought long and hard about their prospects. They were especially concerned about my own future, and concluded that Germany was no place in which to raise a child. This was also the reason why, by 1937, they had not had more children. By the end of the year, Papa and Mama determined to apply for immigration to America.

By the beginning of 1938, Papa sent an inquiry to the US Consulate in Stuttgart, requesting information about needed documents. The reply was a page covered by miniscule print, detailing all the documents that would be required before a visa could be issued. These included the not surprising requests for birth and marriage certificates – in duplicate, plus four photos per person, as well as passports if possible. Most important, a sponsor had to be found in America who could guarantee the refugees' financial well being for a reasonable time after their arrival. A $10 fee (or its equivalent in Reichsmark) was charged for the application, and this had to accompany a short questionnaire providing information for each member of the family seeking to emigrate. A separate document from the consulate warned that, because of the high volume of applications, duplicate submissions of the personal questionnaire might result in extra delays. If the forms were not received by the end of July 1938 (by which time they were likely to be assigned a waiting number of 7700 or higher), then the affidavit guaranteeing financial aid in the US was not to be filed until after that date. Papa sent the forms, documents, and funds off on April 23, 1938.

Fortunately, obtaining an affidavit was not difficult. Ilse – now Elsie – was able to contact a very distant relative in New York, Harry Hyman, who was financially able and morally committed to issuing affidavits for as many German Jewish refugees as possible. The document stipulated that he would be responsible for our welfare – housing and work – once we arrived in the US, so that we would not be a burden on the government. The affidavit, notarized by an attorney in New York, arrived in Kenzingen within a month and on April 15 was forwarded to the consulate; a genealogical document indicating our relation to Harry Hyman was also sent.

Thereupon a series of exchanges took place between the consulate and Papa: The consulate informed him that the guarantee statement was not sufficient; so on June 7, an additional guarantee was sent from New York. Two weeks later, the consulate notified Papa that better, official proof of our guarantor's income and assets were needed. This was finally sent in on July 30. Over the next two weeks, each mail delivery brought with it the slight hope of an answer from the consulate, and each mail delivery brought further disappointment. Papa finally traveled in person to Stuttgart to make inquiries, only to be told that the consulate had no records of his application! Returning home in great frustration, he wrote a letter to the consulate asking for clarification and for a definite waiting number. Our family was disappointed again and again, with each futile trip to the mail box. Finally, on October 18, Papa again traveled to Stuttgart; this time he was told that our waiting number had been assigned as #1141. The number was considerably lower than we might have hoped and provided a tiny bit of good news.

Our experience in 1938 with the US Consulate illustrates clearly what US policy was with regard to German Jewish refugees. The United States, particularly the State Department, was not eager to welcome thousands of German Jews; anti-semitism was widespread, as was anti-immigration in general. The quotas that had been set in the 1920s were strictly enforced, and the quota for Germany was soon declared filled. Consular officials were instructed to make the immigration process as arduous as possible, and to delay as long as they could.

The little optimism raised by the low waiting number was shattered by Kristallnacht and by the consulate's decision not to process visas in ascending order of waiting number from low to high, but rather the be more haphazard and process some of the higher numbers first. With Papa in Dachau and the promised release if we could prove we wished to leave Germany, Mama desperately telegrammed the US consulate inquiring about the status of our application. In answer, she was told that Hyman's "tax payment receipt" was missing. She immediately cabled Hyman in New York, asking him to supply the missing document. The consulate sent no confirmation, but Papa was released from Dachau on the basis of the documentation we had accumulated.

The consulate remained silent about our prospects for emigration. Papa again went to Stuttgart in January 1939, and was stonewalled again. A month later, in desperation, he even tried to write a letter in English and sent it via registered mail:

> *Dear Sir!*
>
> *Why don't I get any answer? I have the low number of 1141. I was there – in Stuttgart – about three weeks ago without having got any information. A lot of letters, I sent, were not answered. My papers are, as I know, all-right. Therefore I beg the Honorable Consul to give me that answer I have to wait for.*
>
> *I am most respectfully yours*

The answer to this letter was also silence. Weeks of agonizing waiting went by. On April 7 another letter – in German – followed, again to the consulate. It detailed the entire process and timetable to that point and again begged for information in case more documents were needed. Return postage was included to encourage an answer. Like all the previous letters, it generated no reply.

Life in Kenzingen became ever more difficult. Since Jews were no longer allowed to own real property, the family house had to be sold considerably below its value. The family was able to continue living in it by paying monthly rent to its new owners. The store, which was forced to close in December of 1938, was finally sold in March 1939. By then, its value had fallen from over 50,000 Mark to only 2,000 Mark, and it carried an outstanding debt of 5,000 Mark. The Nazis also assessed fines on all Jews after Kristallnacht (*Judenvermoegensabgabe)* to help pay for the clean up after the damage created by the pogroms. Papa sold twelve silver serving pieces for 840 Mark to raise the cash. Additional cash for daily living expenses was obtained through the sale of various household items. First to go were baby furnishings and clothing – crib, changing table, crib sheets and blankets. Then some other household items, including the piano, were sold. Savings accounts were frozen by the Nazis, and, in any case, were being carefully protected by Papa and Mama against future emergencies and to use for our potential emigration.

Our social life became non-existent. Villagers mostly turned away if we were in the street. They certainly feared to invite us into their homes, even if they might have been willing to be seen with Jews. It became dangerous for me to play in the street in front of the house, and I relied almost completely on my parents and grandparents for entertainment. Books were read over and over, and I often played *Mensch Aergere Dich Nicht* (Parchesi) with Mama. Problem was, I cried when I lost, but I also cried when I won since then Mama lost! The adults played cards with each other – a substitute for the popular card games that Opa and Papa had played so often with friends in the village. After Kristallnacht, the piano in our living room stood silent and, as noted, was eventually sold. One of the few contacts in Kenzingen outside the immediate family was Fraulein Roederer, who had lived for a time in England and was hired by my parents to teach them some English. She must have been a brave soul to continue into the late 1930s her contacts with the denounced Jews. I assume that these contacts were discretely undertaken after dark. She even gave them a farewell gift as souvenir, a small German/English dictionary, which proved a valuable aid in the first years in America.

In February of 1939, the Nazis decreed that every Jew must obtain an identity card. This act was partly a way of then allowing Germany to issue passports to its stateless Jews, and partly at the urging of the Swiss government, which hoped to use the ID cards as a way of identifying and discriminating against Jews trying to cross over its borders. At the same time, the ID cards indicated most prominently another Nazi form of harassment of Germany's Jews. All Jewish men had had to adopt "Israel" as their middle name, and all women to use "Sarah." After all, the Nazi reasoning was, all Jews are alike so there is no need for them to have distinctive names. Papa, as his ID card attests, became Siegfried Israel Dreifuss, Mama was Gretel Sarah Dreifuss, and I, Alice Sarah Dreifuss. We each had our own card, with a large yellow "J" imprinted on the cover. Each card included a picture of the

Identification card of Siegfried Israel Dreifuss, and of Gretel Sarah Dreifuss, 1939

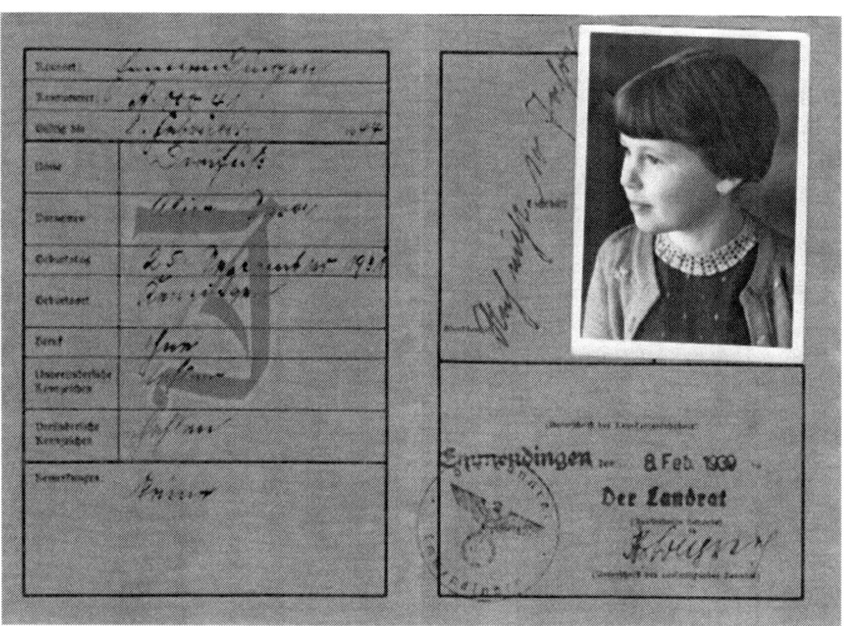

Identification card of Alice Sarah Dreifuss, 1939

individual, photographs carefully taken according to regulations, with backlighting and three-quarter view – to make each person's nose as prominent as possible. As one observer pointed out, the ID cards were hardly necessary; one had only to look at the haunted, terrorized look on the faces of these people to realize that they were Jews. I have a very distinct memory of that photo session. When I went before the camera, I behaved as I'd been taught – I smiled. The photographer promptly scolded me, "This is no time for smiling!"

Although Jews were certainly singled out for extraordinary persecution, life under the Nazi regime was difficult for many of the villagers. They lived in fear of being reported to authorities for the slightest infringement of the law, especially if that involved helping Jews. Spies were everywhere and any disrespect for Nazis was quickly noted and sooner or later punished. Moreover, into the spring and summer of 1939 the villagers had the added fear of impending war. Propaganda prepared the way, as did air raid drills during which tear gas bombs were exploded in the streets to assure that all took shelter. Even we few Jews in the village were expected to go to an air raid shelter, and I can still remember the smell of the tear gas as we hurried across the street into the Englers' basement.

Because of restrictions on when and where we could shop, food became scarce, and we were grateful to the few neighbors who occasionally came to the back door with a basket of fruit or vegetables or some eggs. We were still able to buy basic necessities, but had little money for anything else. Kosher meat became unobtainable, so our diet was basically vegetarian. Very occasionally, a wandering *schochet* (Jew trained in proper ritual slaughter of fowl and animals) would appear in Kenzingen. We would find a chicken to be slaughtered and thus have meat for a day. Chicken remains a treat for me to this day.

Somehow, Oma also managed to continue to raise a goose in our courtyard. It was properly killed for the last Pesach ever to be held in our Kenzingen home – in April of 1939. As usual, we expected that Uncle Max and Aunt Gretel from Berlin and Uncle Julius and Aunt Meta from Dusseldorf would join us for the Seder. Fortunately, travel for Jews was still relatively unrestricted at the time. By then, Uncle Adolf had fled to France, since his outspoken opposition to Hitler made it much too dangerous for him to remain in Germany. Imagine our astonishment when, that night, after all had assembled and prepared to begin the Seder service, Uncle Adolf climbed over the back fence to join us for the festivities! Oma and Opa were terrified that he would be discovered and bring the Gestapo down on the whole family; but they were also so grateful to have the entire family reunited, as we had been in better times. The Seder was held without mishap, and Adolf vanished again two days later. I wonder how many of those sitting around that Seder table recognized that it might be the last time that we would all be together or even see each other.

Shortly after Pesach and Easter, the new school year began. By now, Jewish children were forbidden in any public school, even in separate rooms. So the Jewish School in Freiburg was forced to leave the Lessing Schule to find new quarters in the small Jewish community building that was located near the synagogue but had escaped the flames of *Kristallnacht*. I was happy to return to school after a very long unwanted vacation from November 1938 to April 1939. Our teachers tried very hard to continue our lessons as if we were on a normal schedule. And somehow, my grandparents managed to create a semblance of normalcy at their apartment as well.

I went home for summer vacation in July, not realizing that I wouldn't return in a few weeks. In June, the mail had finally brought the letter that had been awaited for so long. My parents were notified that their visa number had finally been cleared, that they were to appear before the consulate in Stuttgart on July 12 prior to being authorized for immigration to America. We traveled to Stuttgart for the consular review and physical examinations, an excursion I remember well since I had never been so far from home.

The appearance at the consulate necessitated a spate of paper work. Papa immediately wrote to the USS Steamship Co. to inquire about the availability of space on ships going to America. The quick reply indicated that space was plentiful on the USS Harding, sailing from Hamburg on August 15. Tickets were 111.50 Mark for third class passage per adult (the exchange rate at the time was 2.5 Mark to the $1); children were free if in the same stateroom. Taxes, boarding fees, and meal costs added another 72 Mark per person. That passage was so easily available suggests the difficulty Jews had in obtaining permission to immigrate to America. The number of Jews eagerly trying to leave Germany at the time should have made tickets very hard to get; but American officials did their utmost to slow the process.

We applied for passports and were issued them on August 1, good for one year, and not renewable. Our leaving was, after all, helping fulfill Hitler's plan to make Germany *Judenrein*. But before all was set, Papa was notified that he still owed some taxes, even though he had already paid his annual tax and assessment and had no income from the store. There was no appeal, and he paid the additional tax. Other expenses in the amount of 450 Mark included travel costs to Stuttgart and Hamburg (where we were to board the ship) and a foreign exchange fee in the amount of 160 Mark assessed of Jews leaving Germany. All of these funds had to be requested from officials in charge of Papa's frozen bank account, like all Jewish accounts, and required countless paperwork, at least in triplicate.

Final preparations for departure began as early as June, and included selling more household items and then arranging to have basic furniture, clothing, and goods packed for shipping. A large wooden crate – a "lift"

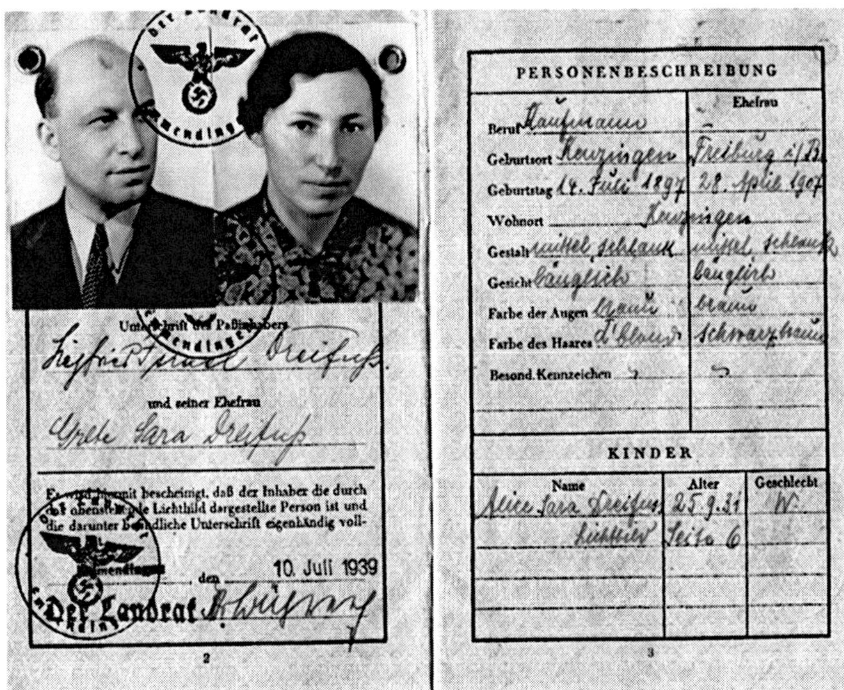

Unterschrift des Paßinhabers

und seiner Ehefrau

Es wird hiermit bescheinigt, daß der Inhaber die durch das obenstehende Lichtbild dargestellte Person ist und die darunter befindliche Unterschrift eigenhändig vollzogen hat.

Emmendingen, den 10. Juli 1939

Der Landrat

2

PERSONENBESCHREIBUNG

		Ehefrau
Beruf	Kaufmann	–
Geburtsort	Kenzingen	Freiburg i/Br.
Geburtstag	19. Juli 1897	28. April 1907
Wohnort	Kenzingen	
Gestalt	mittel, schlank	mittel, schlank
Gesicht	länglich	länglich
Farbe der Augen	braun	braun
Farbe des Haares	d.blond	schwarzbraun
Besond. Kennzeichen	–	–

KINDER

Name	Alter	Geschlecht
Alice Sara Dreifuss	25.9.31	W.
Lichtbild	Seite 6	

3

Passport, 1939

– was erected in the back courtyard, and everything we planned to ship was packed into it – the art deco bedroom furniture, the heavily carved dining table and chairs, a sideboard, dishes, cooking utensils, winter clothing, and pictures. Transportation for the lift, from Kenzingen to Rotterdam and then eventually to New York, cost 1,200 Mark, paid in advance, for a cargo valued at about 10,000 Mark. Everything in the lift was carefully inventoried, with copies sent to the office in charge of foreign dealings in Karlsruhe. Rules regarding what could be taken overseas were carefully spelled out and had to be followed. Nothing of real value could be shipped, including gold and silver jewelry, diamonds and pearls; exceptions were wedding rings and watches for personal use.

We were allowed to take only one steamer trunk with us on board the ship, no valuables, and the equivalent of $5 in cash per person. The trunk was packed with the clothing most necessary for the trip, but also included a packet of documents that my parents thought might be useful in their new lives in America, a very few items of sentimental value, and a small silver sugar spoon (that apparently escaped official notice) and heavy iron food mill overlooked when the lift was packed. From among all my toys, I was allowed to take along only a stuffed animal and a tiny doll in a wicker basket.

The entire process of leaving entailed an immense number of letters to the bank where assets were frozen, to the foreign affairs officials, to the shipping company in charge of sending items by freighter, and to the shipping line to arrange our own transportation. Requests and decisions often took several exchanges and often entailed detailed sets of regulations from officials in Kenzingen and several cities in the area. Enormous patience was required at a time when speed seemed essential and life in Kenzingen became daily more difficult. Hitler may have wanted to rid Germany of its Jews, but the Nazis in no way made the process of leaving easy.

Grandparents Anna and Sigmund Valfer, Freiburg, 1939

In preparation for our leaving, both sets of grandparents had their pictures taken, for who knew when the Hitler madness would pass and we would be reunited. It was especially important for them to feel that Alicele (little Alice) would not forget what they looked like. We boarded the train for Hamburg, from where we subsequently sailed on August 15, 1939. The final trauma of parting is hard to imagine. Our little family was the lynchpin of both the Freiburg and Kenzingen grandparents. We left them with slim hope of reunion and great fear about the future, both for them in Nazi Germany and for us in an unknown land.

Grandparents Louis and Lina Dreifuss, Kenzingen, 1939

Aunt Bertha Dreifuss, 1939

Imagine Dancing at a Time Like This

Our third class cabin on the USS Harding was below the water line and tiny. It must also have been near a galley, since the smell of food permeated the space (not always pleasant once we were seasick!). But I was delighted to be able to claim the upper bunk.

Alice and French playmate, Le Havre, August, 1939

Given the circumstances under which we were traveling, the trip was very pleasant. I finally had the freedom to roam on my own and was happy to explore the third class decks and lounge. All of us delighted in being able to eat a varied menu after the restrictions of the last years. I was amazed to be able to get apple juice for breakfast every day – *Most* (apple cider) had been a seasonal treat – and often asked for an extra glass to take with me on deck. Since so many of the passengers were Jewish refugees, kosher food was an option on board, and my parents happily chose it. Mama and Papa particularly enjoyed having kosher meat and cold cuts that tasted of "home." I generally preferred the home fried potatoes!

The ship stopped in Le Havre to load on supplies. This gave us all a welcome chance to go ashore and stretch our legs in the waterside park. What a treat for me to be able to play safely outdoors. Playing nearby was another little girl in a pretty flowered dress and wide-brimmed straw hat. She was quietly bouncing a ball and must have noticed me watching her. Before long, we threw the ball to each other, wordlessly, since she spoke only French and I spoke only German. But the international language of childhood play was enough for us to spend a very pleasant hour together.

Alice aboard USS Harding August, 1939

The ship also stopped in Southampton and off the coast of Ireland, near Cork. We couldn't disembark at these stops, but the USS Harding did take on supplies and made contact with a mail boat. To my surprise, a small package was delivered to us from Switzerland. Knowing

Switzerland as the source of good chocolate, I eagerly anticipated opening the package and sampling the contents. What a disappointment to find that it contained no chocolate at all, but only some gold jewelry! My parents had arranged to have some family jewelry and a few old gold crowns from teeth smuggled out of Germany – possibly in some of the furniture my Opa had reupholstered – to relatives in Switzerland. These items were to be forwarded to us on the ship. The gold was a kind of insurance, should Papa not get work soon enough to support the family. Fortunately, we were never that strapped for funds, and my Oma's gold watch, which I treasured so much, and other lovely pieces are still among our family heirlooms.

From Ireland, the sea voyage continued uninterrupted for nine more days until we reached New York. Our routine on board was broken only by an occasional safety drill, which brought us all on deck dressed in life jackets. My own pleasure in the freedom of the ship was compromised a little by the toothache I developed a few days before landing. We decided to wait until New York to see a dentist or get other help.

Evenings were often spent in the lounge with a band. Despite all their concerns, Mama and Papa were beguiled by the music and danced. The beat of the "Beer Barrel Polka" is firmly associated in my memory with that trip. Later, especially with hindsight about the terrible events to follow, Mama wondered how she could possibly have danced at such a difficult time. The eleven days at sea constituted an incredible hiatus of calm -- a respite from the agonies of Nazism and a prelude to the difficulties we were bound to face in our new home.

Debarkation formalities were fast and easy. Processing took place in the grand salon of the first class. A quick check of documents, not even a stamp in our passport, and we were free to disembark. Ilse – we were quickly told to call her Elsie now that we were in America – met us at the dock and whisked us off to the apartment she'd arranged.

Inexperienced When They Came

Our new home was located in Washington Heights, the core area of German Jewish refugees. English was barely heard in the streets; shops catered to German tastes, from delicatessen to butchers to bakeries; signs were in German. The synagogues in the area used German Jewish *nussach* (order of service) and sermons were preached in German. Our apartment turned out to be two rooms off a long hall. The place was full of over-stuffed furniture, dark paneling, musty odors. No sun reached the windows. How dismayed Mama and Papa must have been to realize that this would be our home, even as they were grateful for the safe haven it provided.

For me, the first order of business was to take care of my toothache. Elsie found a dentist who agreed to see me Monday morning. I went reluctantly, accompanied by Mama and Elsie. The dentist said that since the ache was in a baby tooth, the easiest procedure would be just to pull the tooth; another would take its place soon enough. I was terrified. The dentist, simply reached in my mouth to pull the tooth out – no novocaine or anesthetic. I resisted, and bit down on the hand propping my mouth open with as much force as I could. I often wondered afterwards if the poor dentist was scarred for life! But the tooth came out and my ache disappeared.

With only $15 to our name, Mama and Papa, of course, immediately tried to find work. Jobs were scarce since the United States was still suffering the lingering effects of the Depression. Mama was fortunate (if that's the right word) to get hired immediately as a cleaning woman in one of the apartment houses in the block. Papa went to HIAS (Hebrew Immigrant Aid Society) to see if they had any work available. That required some paper work and time, but he was told to come back the following week.

At the end of our first week in New York, Labor Day weekend, Elsie appeared with a treat for all. She had obtained tickets to "The Wizard of Oz" at the Capitol Theater. Not that we had any idea of what the movie was or why it was so special. We went and I remember understanding not a word, but enjoying the amazing Technicolor. I was especially enchanted by the appearance of Judy Garland on stage in her checked dress and ruby slippers. What a contrast that fantasy world was to the reality of our airless apartment and grim prospects for work and to the terrible war that was already underway overseas.

The following Tuesday, school began for the year, and Mama took me to the public school that served the Washington Heights area. The huge red brick box with its cement yard looked like a monster to me. The long corridors, many doors, hundreds of children were totally intimidating, especially after the confined school space and tiny classes that I'd attended in Freiburg. None of the administrators or teachers spoke anything but English to us, even though the school was in a heavily German-speaking neighborhood. Somehow, Mama made them understand that I needed to be enrolled and that I would be eight years old in a few weeks. She had my birth certificate and report cards from Germany to prove it. So I was placed in third grade, shown to the room, and left to manage while Mama went to work.

Then, as now, school days all over America began with the Pledge of Allegiance to the flag. All the class stood up – except me. I'd been taught that the flag was a Nazi symbol and meant only disaster for Jews like me. "Avoid looking at it, and don't salute it," I'd been told. I remembered that lesson in the New York classroom and remained in my seat. The teacher saw only inexplicable disobedience and immediately sent me to an empty room, to think about how disrespectful I'd been. I was only bewildered.

That evening Mama and Papa explained the difference between the flags in Germany and those in my new country, and I went back to school the next day feeling a bit better. School went more smoothly until the class turned to the day's arithmetic lesson – long division. With my sporadic and interrupted schooling in Freiburg, I had only progressed to simple division and had no idea how to tackle these new problems. Back to the empty room I went, mortified and more bewildered than ever. To cap the events of the week, Friday was assembly day at school and all children were required to wear white blouses/shirts and dark blue skirts/pants. Of course, I had neither, and once again was sent out of the class. How I hated that school!

Fortunately, rescue was on the way. During the week, Papa had returned to HIAS and been informed that a family in Bennington, Vermont was looking for a "couple" (husband to serve as butler, gardener, chauffeur and wife as cook and housemaid) and would be willing to accept a child as well. We'd never heard of Vermont, and hiring on as servants seemed a hard way to earn a living, a far cry from the kind of life my parents had known. In addition, going so far away meant breaking the close support that Elsie had been able to give us. But there were benefits. The $25 per month salary would not have to be spent on room and board, since these were provided by the family, and it would take us out of New York. None of us was happy with the situation in the city, and my parents realized quickly that, if they were to be Americanized, it would be easier to do so away from Washington Heights. After considerable thought, Papa and Mama accepted the position, and agreed to move to Bennington immediately. I was delighted not to have to go back to that awful school.

The Verblows lived in a grand house just up a hill from the center of Bennington. The wide lawn was surrounded by trees and plantings, and a play house perched at the far end of the garden for use by their two children, Vicky (age 10) and David (age 5). The top floor of the three-story house had been outfitted as servants' quarters: two bedrooms and a bath, with simple basic furnishings. A stairway led down from these rooms to the back hallway of the second floor and then directly into the kitchen on the first floor. It's ironic that in many ways our living situation in Bennington echoed that in Kenzingen. Both apartments were on the third floor and were accessed by back stairs. For me, this

Verblow house, Bennington, VT, 1940.
Arrow indicates "our room"

was a perfectly normal order of doing things, but for my parents, it must have been a difficult and frightening adjustment.

During the next few weeks, Mama and Papa learned what was expected of a "couple." For Mama, the kitchen was headquarters. Each morning she cleaned the house and, in consultation with Mrs. Verblow, planned the meals for the day. Many of the foods were great mysteries to her, both because she had no idea what the English words meant and because she had never cooked them before. So the little red German-English dictionary was propped on the window sill, next to a copy of "The Settlement House Cookbook" (on loan from the Verblows), and Mama went from one to the other as she cooked her way through the menu. Of course, she also added her own familiar recipes, often much to the delight of Mr. Verblow, who hated spinach until Mama served it in our traditional style. Nonetheless, Mama must have felt very insecure, and in one of her first letters back to her mother, she asked for a series of cookie recipes. The letter was quickly answered, and the scraps of thin airmail paper on which they were written were treasured for years. Most of the time, Mama could wear ordinary dresses, but when the family entertained, she was expected to wear a maid's uniform. She was outfitted in a black dress with a white frilly apron to denote her status.

Papa divided his time among outdoor work, the family car, and serving as butler. He had to get work clothes for the manual garden work, and he wore a chauffeur's cap when driving Mrs. Verblow on errands. For me, the most impressive uniform was what he was expected to wear while serving the nightly dinners. Since dinner was a formal affair in the dining room, Papa had to wear black trousers, a white jacket, and black bow tie. A white linen napkin was carefully draped over his arm. He looked grand in the outfit, and I loved seeing him dressed in it; for him it must have been a mockery of the top hat and tuxedo he wore to the opera. But the most significant change for Papa occurred immediately on our arrival in Bennington. "We can't call you Siegfried," Mrs. Verblow declared, "so from now on, you'll be Fred." And he was, for the rest of his life, even to Mama.

I was quickly enrolled in public school in Bennington, a kindly and welcoming place. Because of my lack of English, I was placed in second grade, in the hope that I would learn the language quickly and be able to move on to the appropriate grade soon. Again, I was in an all-English environment, but without the strict atmosphere of New York and with very understanding teachers. In fact, I began to function in English soon enough, and after the winter break was moved to third grade, with children my own age. Once I was fluent in English, I became a regular at the local library and devoured books as fast as I could borrow them. They were an excellent substitute for the friends I had not made. I think I was too foreign for other children to warm up to me easily, and I myself was wary of trusting other children after my experiences in Germany. On top of that, I was Jewish at a time when anti-semitism was very common. When the library had a reading contest during vacation, I was warned that it would be inappropriate for me to win it since I was a Jew. Did I feel the echoes of the hatred we'd left behind?

Still, my first year in America was good, and the Verblows were quite considerate of me. My birthday came shortly after our arrival in Bennington. There wasn't much Mama and Papa could do to celebrate it, but the Verblows gave me a plaid raincoat and a set of watercolors – my first American clothes and my first art supplies. I was also considered a part of the family when Christmas was celebrated. Like Vicky and David, I hung a stocking by the fireplace and found presents under the tree. I learned Christmas carols and thoroughly enjoyed the holiday. Occasionally, since I played with Vicky, I was invited to join the family for dinner in the dining room. How I loved to have my Papa serve me in full formal style!

Mama and Papa found friends in Bennington – two German Jewish families who had moved there several years before our arrival. Julius Manes was a doctor; he and his wife were particularly helpful to us and quickly drew us into their activities on Papa's and Mama's days off – every Thursday afternoon and every other Sunday afternoon. Since their house was just across the street from the school, it was also a haven for me when I felt particularly forlorn.

With such a full work schedule in a strange house, it wasn't possible to observe Shabbat, or, of course, to keep kosher. But we did ask to have the High Holy Days off and attended the small synagogue that served Bennington's Jews. Since the Verblows knew nothing of the holidays, no provisions were made for us to have special meals. My parents long remembered the unusual dinner they had before *Kol Nidrei* (before beginning the day-long *Yom Kippur* fast) of two hot dogs and some potatoes. Papa always maintained that was the easiest fast he ever had.

Sometime during that winter, we had a week's vacation. Very generously, the Verblows gave us one of the family cars for the trip to New York. They had apparently gained a great deal of confidence in Papa's driving skills to allow this. I have very little memory of that trip, which was primarily spent with Elsie. I personally had only terrible memories of time in New York and was happy to go back to Bennington at the end of the week. The trip did, however, add to our English vocabulary. We were curious when we saw signs along the Vermont roads that read "Frost Heaves," and had no idea what that meant. When the car bounced over the bump in the road, we quickly learned!

Of course, we tried as much as possible to keep in touch with family in Freiburg and Kenzingen. Even air mail was excruciatingly slow, and it was extremely frustrating to have to wait up to a month for a letter exchange – two weeks in each direction. Often we wrote to Oma and

Opa in Freiburg, and they then sent the letter on to Oma and Opa in Kenzingen. In turn, Kenzingen news was often relayed via Freiburg. But in late January 1940, a letter came directly from Kenzingen, with the sad news that Oma had died. She had apparently had a heart attack and died quickly and peacefully. Opa described her last few hours:

> *"On Friday evening we sat quietly together, and nothing seemed unusual for Mother. She went to bed around 9:30. Occasionally, she complained of a shortness of breath, but had two such attacks in the past. When she complained that she couldn't seem to breathe, I called Aunt Sophie (Sophie Epstein, Oma's sister) and she went to fetch the doctor. He came and gave Oma three injections, but they didn't work, and around 11:30 she passed quietly and softly away. We will not complain and let her rest in peace. Dear God has so ordained it, and we all must follow God's will, we all must follow the same path.*
>
> *"For me, this time is particularly difficult, since we were together for such a long and satisfying time. Now we must pray to God to give us all good health. Dear Aunt Sophie is here with us; you know that Aunt Bertha (Opa's sister, who lived with him) isn't doing so well. So the three of us will have to support one another, and I will strive to maintain our unity and peace. We are comforted that Mother died as a good wife, a good mother, and a good Jew, and that she leaves behind a good husband. That is particularly comforting in these times. Her worries about the current times disturbed her so often.*
>
> *"Her heart glowed at the thoughts of her only grandchild; she had so much pleasure from you letters, and told everyone how well little Alicele was doing in school. I pray that you, dear Alicele, will always remember your grandmother. And I pray that you, dear Siegfried and dear Gretel will be strong and accept what fate brings. That is what God wants. You, dear Siegfried, will observe*

the year of mourning for your dear mother, as is required of a good Jewish son."

The letter went on to indicate that Julius and Meta were in Kenzingen and that they all went to the synagogue in Emmendingen on the Saturday following Oma's death. Oma was buried in the new Jewish cemetery in Emmendingen. In many ways, the letter indicated an amazing continuity of Jewish life in Germany as late as 1940, which permitted travel, religious services, and religious burials. It's also amazing that the doctor in Kenzingen felt free and was willing to come to the house to treat Oma, after the several years of boycott and restrictions that had pushed Jews so far toward the margins of society and had made them so reviled by many.

Alice with parents, Bennington, VT, April 1940

Papa followed the letter's instructions. He observed eleven months of mourning -- no music, no entertainment. Given the scant free time in Bennington, this was not especially hard to follow. A major highlight of the months that followed was Elsie's visit in the spring. We had a few extra hours of free time in honor of the visit. Best of all from my point of view, Elsie brought me my first really "American" outfit – a maroon pleated skirt with matching jacket and a pink blouse. The jacket had little gold stars and a crescent moon on its lapels. Elsie even supplied a matching maroon hat. I felt so special in these clothes and wore them at every possible "special occasion."

By late spring, we had all become quite comfortable in English, I considerably more than my parents. Their facility in their new language was a key factor in their decision to leave Bennington. The situation with the Verblows was not pleasant at best, and at worst resulted in a very constrained life, including barely enough food. So in August 1940, my parents indicated that they were terminating their employment and asked for a letter of reference. The few lines indicated that they were "sober and industrious" and "had little experience when they came." We packed our few belongings and headed back to New York.

Connections and Change

In September 1940, we found ourselves back in New York, and, inevitably, back in Washington Heights. And, alas, I found myself enrolled in the same school that had been so dreadful for me a year earlier. This time I felt more at ease, but certainly not happy. My great consolation was the promise that we would be able to go to the World's Fair, whose pylon and hemisphere I had seen when Elsie took me to the top of the Empire State Building.

Alice with Elsie Mayer, New York, June 1940

Once again, Mama and Papa had to look for work. Papa immediately reported to HIAS, as he had a year earlier, to see about job possibilities. He was more optimistic this time since he not only knew some English, but the economy was beginning to improve and jobs were somewhat more plentiful. HIAS searched their files and, within a few days indicated that a factory in Philadelphia was seeking workers. Papa agreed that we would be willing to relocate.

Walking back to Washington Heights from the HIAS office, he was pleasantly surprised to encounter a *landsman* (fellow countryman) from Germany – Gus Johl, who had lived with his family in Rust, a village very close to Kenzingen. Gus and his family had left Germany about a year before us, and he had moved to Groton, Connecticut, under the sponsorship of a distant relative, Max Johl. Max owned a small factory and a very large piece of land at Trails Corner, on the outskirts of Groton. Gus served as a plant manager and lived with his sister Sophie in a small house on the Johl property.

As Gus and Papa caught up with each other's history over the past year, Gus became more and more interested in our situation. He told Papa that one of his missions in New York was to find domestic servants to work in the Johl household. They had recently had a baby and wanted household help. Wouldn't we like to apply for that job? It would be an excellent position, since we would be near friends, and Gus was ready to vouch for the pleasant atmosphere of the Johl household. Of course, he had to contact them to see if they would be willing to take on a couple with a child – if we were interested.

Papa and Mama discussed the offer. They recognized that they had very few options. They had no savings, since the little they had earned in Bennington had to be spent first on supplying us with the clothing necessary for the cold Vermont winter and second on providing some support for parents left behind in Germany, mostly in the form of packages. By then, they were also quite certain that the lift full of our furniture was unlikely to arrive in New York any time in the foreseeable future. The freighter on which it was to be shipped was stopped at the outbreak of the war in 1939 and rerouted to Rotterdam, Holland, where it had been held up. With a choice between starting fresh in totally unknown Philadelphia or going to Groton, where we had friends, the decision was clear, even though it meant more work as servants. Papa told Gus that we were willing to take the position.

Gus had checked with Janet and Max Johl in Groton and they were agreeable to having the three of us. The arrangement would be similar to the one in Bennington: We would live in the servants' quarters on the third floor of the Johl house. Papa would serve as butler, chauffeur, and gardener; Mama as housekeeper and cook. I would go to public school along with the two Johl boys, Peter (age 13) and John (age 10). The smallest Johl – little Janet (age 6 months) – was not to be Mama's responsibility. As before, we were to have every Thursday afternoon and every other Sunday off. An improvement over Bennington was the increase in the monthly salary to $90.

Once agreement was reached, we packed up again and in short order found ourselves in the Johl family car en route to "Konnektikut"?? I was greatly disappointed that we left New York before I could go to the World's Fair. We arrived in Groton at night. Gus ushered us to the front door of a very large house to announce our arrival. But we'd been anticipated by Peggy, the Johl's very large and gentle collie dog. Unfortunately, she greeted us by jumping up on and totally terrifying me. I had become very afraid of dogs (because of their use by the Nazis?), and I never did make friends with Peggy, though I came to tolerate her over time. (I'm still afraid of dogs!)

The situation at the Johl's was far better than the one with the Verblows, though there were some parallels. Again, we lived in a household with a tenuous Jewish connection (through Max Johl) but that observed Christian rituals. In fact, Janet Johl was a practicing Christian Scientist who, several months after our arrival, horrified Mama by living by her beliefs. When Peter stepped on a rusty nail, she refused to seek medical care or get him a tetanus shot, but simply prayed for him to get better. (Fortunately, he did.)

At the Johls, who were a good deal less formal than the Verblows, we were treated almost as part of the family. Mama and Papa seldom had to wear uniforms, though Papa was still summoned to serve in the dining room by a tap on the buzzer discreetly hidden under the carpet at Mrs. Johl's seat. Food was plentiful and Mama's cooking most appreciated. My parents were naturally more comfortable since they could now function reasonably well in English. I had stopped speaking German altogether.

I loved the Johl house. Janet Johl had an extensive doll collection that I was occasionally allowed to help her arrange. I was also fascinated by Max Johl's collection of minerals, which he displayed and lighted so that they glowed in the dark. I was introduced there to mah jongg and the phonograph (the wind-up variety). Mama managed to get me lessons on their baby grand piano – until it became clear that I had no inclination to practice and that I was no budding Horowitz. But I did learn the rudiments of reading music. Mama never touched the piano to play -- the Nazis had destroyed that desire completely – but she and Papa loved music and listened to the classical radio stations whenever possible. They even had an opportunity to attend a concert, when the Johls were unable to use their tickets to a New London concert by the Boston Symphony Orchestra. Janet loaned Mama one of her evening gowns (concerts then were quite formal affairs) and Papa looked dapper in his suit. They drove to the concert in the Johl's Packard for an evening that must have been full of bitter-sweet memories.

Papa drove me to school along with the boys. I was placed in fourth grade, but because of high enrollment was delighted to find myself in a mixed fourth/fifth grade, where I could eavesdrop on the fifth grade lessons when I'd finished my own assignments. That winter, the school produced "A Christmas Carol." Peter Johl had the lead as Scrooge, and I had a bit part as a herald announcing the opening of the play. I went to all the rehearsals and memorized every part of the play. In Groton, I finally began to feel more integrated into school.

My parents must have been very concerned that I was growing up without any Jewish content in my life. It was, of course, impossible to observe *kashrut* (Jewish dietary laws) or Shabbat. Still, my parents were determined that I get at least some Jewish education, and on one of their first Thursdays off, they identified the conservative congregation in New London, Beth El, as an appropriate place for me to go to religious school. Their *minhag* (ritual and service) seemed to match best with the modern Orthodox service of the Freiburg synagogue. A small house on Blackhall Street contained their classrooms, offices, and sanctuary. Rabbi Ruderman was happy to welcome me to the school even though it was clear that I could attend only on Thursdays, and not on Sundays or Tuesdays as the other children my age did. By then, I had forgotten pretty much everything I had learned in the Jewish school in Freiburg, and had to begin almost at the *aleph-bet* (the alphabet). With understanding teachers, I soon caught up with my classmates and was introduced to Hebrew grammar and syntax. We had weekly worksheets to complete, which I soon learned to ignore just like the other students! Still, the weekly sessions laid a foundation for later, more regular instruction.

Hebrew school became a regular feature of my parents' Thursdays off. After preparing dinner to be left for Janet Johl to warm up, we caught a bus from Trails Corner to the center of New London. From there it was an easy walk – a mile or so – to the small synagogue. While I was in Hebrew school, Mama and Daddy explored New London, occasionally went to the movies, and took care of the bureaucratic paper work associated with trying to get a visa for Oma and Opa interned in France (see below). In their walks, they naturally stopped to look over the city's fabric store, probably making lots of mental comparisons with memories of their own store in Kenzingen. The visit was serendipitous because the store was owned by the Linz/Kupfer family – refugees like my parents, who eventually became family friends. I resented being left out of all these interesting doings, but having to be at Hebrew school was sweetened by being able to join my parents for an early supper at New London's Hygienic Restaurant, where my favorite dish was a fried egg sandwich.

On the Johl property stood an old barn that had been renovated as a kind of social hall and was dubbed "The Russian Rooster." The Johls occasionally had large parties there, as they did on Halloween 1940. Everyone had to be in costume, including Mama and Papa, who cooked and served for the occasion. Mama dressed as a goose girl, with a wig of blonde braids and a cardboard goose (designed by Papa) tucked under her arm. Papa was dressed as a Cossack in borrowed boots and loose shirt. It was a happy party, despite the terrible news about the war front in Europe, and even Mama and Papa had a good time. It must have reminded them so much of the gay *Fastnacht* parties they had so loved.

What they didn't know was that the Johls had received news the day before the party of the deportation of all the Jews in Southwest Germany to detention camps in southern France. My parents were told of the deportations the next day and realized that most of our family must have been included in the action. Just as our lives were beginning to take on a semblance of normalcy with time to relax and laugh a little, this news brought us back to the terrible realities of Nazi policies. There was little they could do except wait and hope for more definite word of what had happened and where our family had been taken. Meanwhile, they had a job to do, which they saw as including protecting me from as much unpleasantness and sorrow as possible. They seldom expressed any of their fears in front of me.

Envelope returned to parents after deportation from Kenzingen to Gurs, France, October 1940

The summer of 1941 at Trails Corner was a happy time for me. I often joined the boys at the private beach club to which the family belonged. Like the boys, I took swimming lessons and learned to dive – well enough to earn a diving trophy at the end of the season (the only athletic trophy I'll ever get!). Janet Johl's father, Mr. Pagter came to visit. A courtly gentleman, he took special interest in the children, including me, and in the garden. A favorite ploy of his to keep us youngsters busy was to pay one cent for every Japanese beetle we caught and dropped into jars of kerosene. We became eager collectors. We all enjoyed the extensive vegetable garden planted across the street from the house. Mama was pleased with the gooseberry bushes that enabled her to make pies like those in Kenzingen. We all learned that corn was good to eat and not just cattle fodder. Mama put up water to boil while Papa went across the street to pick armfuls of corn, including some very colorful varieties of Indian corn. At the very end of the season, we helped dig up the last of the potatoes and sat around a bonfire as they roasted.

In September, we were given time off to attend religious services for the High Holy Days in New London. We took the bus into town for Rosh Hashanah, but on Yom Kippur, we walked the several miles to downtown New London. Since I was too young to fast all day, my parents quietly took me to get lunch at a nearby tea room, embarrassed to be seen in a place serving food even though I was the only one eating. To their surprise, several members of the congregation had preceded them and were enjoying their meals!

Christmas was a big event at Trails Corner, as it had been in Bennington. On Christmas Eve, I hung my stocking on the mantel as the boys did, and I found presents waiting for me under the tree when I ran down early on Christmas day. My very favorite gift was a large (two foot) stuffed doll that Janet Johl and Mama had made together. It was my bedtime companion for many years. I also received some hand-me-down ice skates, which I used on the tiny pond on the Johl property.

The year at Trails Corner enabled us to begin feeling at home in the United States. My parents had their dignity restored, even though they remained domestic servants. They recognized continuities in some of the customs and foods to which they'd been accustomed in Germany, while also adapting to American ways. Orange juice became a breakfast staple, and Papa became "Daddy" and developed a fondness for corn flakes. We all became much more fluent in English and remained cautiously optimistic about the situation in Europe, now focused on France as well as Germany.

We continued to follow the events in Europe and became increasingly concerned about America's role. In fact, the country was gearing up for war despite strong isolationist and pro-Nazi factions. We were made painfully aware of the process at the end of September. Max Johl was an officer in the Army Reserves and was given notice that his unit was being called into active duty. Since he was to be stationed in the Chicago area, this meant that the house at Trails Corner would have to be closed, and that we would lose our position. Mr. Johl arranged for Daddy to get a job as night watchman at his factory in Groton, and my parents determined to move to New London, where Mama had some opportunities of finding work and where we could be closer to a Jewish community. Leaving the Johls was one more difficult goodbye and again put us into a new and insecure situation.

"I'm So Thin, You Wouldn't Recognize Me"

In October of 1940, the Nazis tried an experiment to gauge world reaction. They deported the Jews of Baden, Pfalz, and the Saar to internment camps in France. A precedent for such deportations had been established earlier, when Jews of East European citizenship living in Germany had been unceremoniously rounded up and sent over the border of Germany into Poland, and when some 22,000 Jews of Alsace were sent into unoccupied France after the Nazi take-over of northern France. But this was the first time that persons who were German-born were deported to camps in another country.

As the Nazis expected, the world press barely noticed. Attention was focused on the war itself, and even Jewish communities in the free world muted their reactions. Such lack of outrage emboldened the Nazis to further their persecution of the Jews and to eventually develop the "Final Solution." In histories written of the Second World War and of the Nazi regime the deportations to France received scant attention and, in fact, is most often not cited at all. For Mama and Daddy, it was devastating news.

On October 22, 1940, in the middle of the holiday of Sukkoth, a carefully planned deportation plan was set in motion. Jewish homes in Southwest Germany received "polite" visits from the Gestapo, announcing that they were not to leave their homes and to make themselves ready for a journey. They were to take with them necessities to last several days, but no more than 50 kg. per adult and 30 kg. per child. Many were advised to take with them supplies of food. Families were also told they could take with them no more than 100 mark. The Gestapo indicated they would return within an hour. They did not indicate where Jews were to be sent or for how long they would be away, but the action was done quietly so as to keep the deportees as docile as possible. Many thought they would be absent for only a few days or a couple of weeks at most. Despite the degradations they had continually experienced over the past five years, long-term deportation was beyond the imagination of most. They carefully locked their homes as they left.

In Kenzingen, by October 1940, my immediate family were the only Jews still resident. Thus, three Jews were picked up – my Opa Ludwig Dreifuss, Tante Bertha Dreifuss, and Tante Sophie Epstein, all living together in the house on Brotstrasse. What a wrenching experience it must have been for them, all elderly people, with no sense of security away from the only home they'd ever known. In Freiburg, where many more Jews still lived, my Oma Anna Valfer, Opa Sigmund Valfer, and Uncle Siegfried Mayer (cousin Elsie's father) were among the hundreds of men, women, and children gathered at the central railroad station to await the train that would take them to their unknown destination. They must have derived some small comfort from being with many of their friends.

Long trains of third class passenger cars waited at the main railroad stations, where Jews were first asked to stow their luggage in the baggage cars and then ordered to board and take their seats. As the trains got under way, many feared that their destination was Poland, but as they recognized the names of the towns that flashed by on the stations along the way, they realized that they were, instead, moving south. Trains stopped at Mulhausen in Alsace, where the deportees were told to exchange their 100 mark into French francs (often at a rate well below the posted exchange). In all, the trains took three days and nights (often shunted to side rails while other trains sped by) to reach their destination – Gurs.

Gurs, located in the Pyrenees Mts. of southwestern France about 50 miles from the Spanish border, had been established in April 1939 by the French as an internment camp for defeated Spanish Republican soldiers and others fleeing from Spain to France after the Spanish Civil War. In early 1940, the French also interned there some 4,000 German Jews, whom they had declared "enemy aliens." The camp had only primitive facilities – large wooden barracks that lacked any kinds of furniture, few cooking facilities, and constant shortages of water and food. The barracks were organized into "ilots" (little islands) connected to each other by dirt paths that turned into ankle deep mud during the long rainy season. Only the main road through the camp was paved.

Into this dismal place, the Germans dumped the 7,500 Jews from southwestern Germany. By this time, Germany had occupied northern France, but the south, including the area in which Gurs was located, was under the puppet Vichy regime and staffed by French officials. The Germans failed to notify Vichy that the Jews were coming, so the internment camp, which was marginally supplied at best, was woefully inadequate to receive the thousands of newcomers. It's hard to imagine how anyone, especially the very old and very young, could have survived. Even though the camp was not designed as a "killing camp," during 1940-41, some 800 detainees at Gurs did, in fact, die, and were buried in the camp's cemetery.

Somehow, the newcomers managed to organize the camp, with central kitchens, some rudimentary medical care, schools for children, religious services, and cultural events. In this they received some help from the French authorities and also from some of the people living in the area. Conditions were more fluid and flexible in France than they were in the camps of either Germany or Eastern Europe. Children were regularly smuggled out of the camp to take refuge with French families, in orphanages or in convents, or to be guided over the Pyrenees on foot for safety in Spain. Adults were frequently moved from Gurs to other camps in the region, where they were often used as slave labor. These camps included les Milles – an old tile factory turned into brick factory; Noe and Recebedou, just south of Toulouse; and Rivesaltes, which had been a transit camp for troops in World War I, but which, in 1940-42, was primarily reserved for Jews who had some expectation of emigration. More important, Jews in these various camps were also able to correspond with family overseas, although letters were heavily censored by French and German authorities, and to receive funds from abroad.

As soon as my parents received a telegram with the dreadful news, they initiated whatever actions they could to help my grandparents. The deportation was also documented by the return of a letter that had been sent to my Opa Dreifuss in Kenzingen in May of 1940. It came to us in Groton (the mail followed us from Bennington) toward the end of the year. The envelope showed signs of censorship and carried a small label, "Moved without forwarding address," in both German and French. Except for this envelope, little of the early correspondence with either my grandparents or various agencies in the United States survives, but some chronology can be worked out from the existing documents and from a series of later letters, especially from my grandmother, written during 1941-42.

Avenues of help in America for the interned Jews in France were few, and the process of getting assistance overseas was cumbersome. My parents turned both to official agencies and to family. A natural avenue for help was HIAS, which had helped in our resettlement and was now engaged in "Rescue through Emigration." They served as a clearing house for obtaining information and forms related to the emigration process. In February 1941, they sent us the forms required by the US Commission on Immigration and Naturalization (CIN) to begin the arduous process of obtaining visas for my grandparents. A deposit of $6 was required. Two months later, the CIN had still not responded, and HIAS apparently gave up hope of any action, since they refunded the $6 deposit.

In the meantime, Daddy had also turned to the American Friends Service Committee (AFSC), not for visa assistance, but both to enable my grandparents to be transferred out of Gurs, and also to transfer funds to France to help my grandparents survive while they waited for authorization to emigrate. AFSC was helpful. They served as a conduit for funds from my parents to my grandparents, requiring only $1 fee to cover the costs of the cable. In April, Daddy sent AFSC $47, $30 to be given to Sigmund and Anna Valfer (Freiburg Opa and Oma) and $15 to Ludwig Dreifuss (Kenzingen Opa). At that time, Daddy was also notified that in order to effect a transfer out of Gurs, a guarantee of support would be needed of at least $26 a month. The transfer was not at all certain, but AFSC was willing to try and to notify my Valfer Opa about this.

The funds were augmented for my grandparents from yet another source. Just before we left Kenzingen, our lift which had been sent for transshipment by freighter, had been delayed in Hamburg, and failed to leave Europe before the onset of hostilities in September 1939. The freighter was able to reach Rotterdam, Holland, and there it was stuck. The contents had to be down-loaded and stored (for which we were charged a storage fee). By the spring of 1941, the stored contents could no longer be held, and they were auctioned off. After all the fees were paid, the contents of the lift netted 235 Dutch florins. Daddy asked that the funds be transferred to Gurs, 70 florins to Ludwig Dreifuss, 70 florins to Sigmund Valfer, and 95 florins to Anna Valfer. (Hereafter, when I speak of Oma and Opa, I will be referring to my Valfer grandparents; my Dreifuss Opa will be specified as such.)

Not surprisingly, the process for individuals to transfer from Gurs was not so simple. AFSC notified Daddy that their Marseilles office had received the request and funds, and had notified my grandparents. But more was needed:

> *"It is almost necessary now, however, for the persons themselves to know some people – French Nationals – who will undertake to appeal to the prefects of the departments in which they live on behalf of the internees. Do you know whether your parents-in-law are acquainted with any one in southern France who might arrange for them to live either with them or in the home of someone in the community?"*

Before more contacts could be made in Gurs, the AFSC lost track of Opa's whereabouts. He had been transferred to Camp les Milles, apparently because he was considered still strong enough to serve in the slave labor unit there.

Daddy also took advantage of the family's international dispersion to contact Alfred Faller, a distant cousin, in Zurich, Switzerland. Faller worked for a bank and devoted a considerable portion of his energies and wealth in assisting a wide assortment of relatives and friends who had fallen victim to the Nazis. Although I have none of the correspondence that passed between them during the war years, I do know that as of July of 1941, my parents sent funds to Faller's account in Zurich. During that first half year alone, they sent at least $210 to Switzerland, to be transferred to my grandparents in France. Given a monthly salary of only $90 a month, the sum sent overseas was a substantial part of their earnings during that time. Most of that money seems to have reached my grandparents, since it appears to have kept them healthy enough (allowing them, among other things, to buy food to supplement the camp rations) to survive the first year of deportation.

Exchanges of letters between my parents and grandparents occurred within a short time of the deportation, as did the one-way stream of funds and packages of food and warm clothing, although some of these were routed via Switzerland. Many of the packages failed to arrive or were tampered with en route. For example, three tins of sardines (high calorie and therefore especially welcome) were sent by my Aunt Meta (my father's sister-in-law, who was still living in Dusseldorf, Germany), but only one tin was in the package that reached Oma. Mail was very erratic and letters were often lost before they reached their intended address. Apparently, several of the early letters were never delivered in the United States; the first letter that has survived is dated September 25, 1941. It was written from Gurs by my Oma, especially to note my birthday. She reports that all the immediate family are well (including Oma and Opa, my Dreifuss Opa, Aunt Sofie, and Uncle Siegfried), and also tells about a variety of more distant relatives and friends with whom she has contact, either by mail, word of mouth from others, or personal visits within the camp.

The letter also describes that first Rosh Hashanah away from home:

> *"For* Jontef *(the holidays) I went to the* Kulturbaraque *(a barrack in Gurs set aside for cultural events) and services were very nice. Cantor Israel prayed very movingly and a choir of men and women sang beautifully. After the service, we went to the* Feldgottesdienst *(services held in a large outdoor space), where Rabbi Ausbach gave an*

> *excellent sermon, after which we heard the shofar blown. Among the many hundred people gathered there, I doubt that an eye was dry; at that point I was truly overcome by homesickness."*

A very slow stream of internees were able to leave the camp for safer destinations: some, like Aunt Sofie were able to gain entrance to Switzerland; a few found haven in Cuba; and some heard from the American consulate in Marseilles that their documents were in order and that they were authorized to emigrate to the US. The wait must have seemed endless and the disappointments constant. In the meantime, the internees at Gurs were being shuffled around the various other camps in unoccupied France. By the end of 1941, both my Opa and Uncle Siegfried had been transferred to Camps les Milles, where they were used as laborers making bricks. The separation between my grandparents was very difficult for them to bear. My Dreifuss Opa was transferred to Noe. Other internees were allowed to move out of the camp into a transit hotel in Marseilles if the consulate indicated that their papers were being processed.

By December, both my Valfer grandparents were out of Gurs, my Oma having been transferred to the transit Hotel Bomport in Marseilles upon authorization from the American consulate. One of the real benefits of the change in residence was that my grandfather was allowed two days leave from the brick factory every three weeks, so that he could visit my grandmother in Marseilles. They also managed to communicate on an almost daily basis through letters hand delivered by various internees of Les Milles who were on a different leave schedule. Their new quarters and all the communications they had had with the American consulate caused considerable optimism and hope that they would soon be reunited with us in the United States. As my grandfather wrote in January, "Daily, we await news regarding the trip and regarding the willingness from Washington. I am firmly convinced that we've done all we can, and now simply need to have patience." Rumors about procedures to simplify and speed up the emigration process circulated among the internees and fueled their sense of hope.

By the end of the winter, as the weather improved, hope eroded. Mail was very erratic and many of the letters sent in either direction between my parents and grandparents failed to arrive. My Oma wrote that a large bundle of letters arrived at the hotel from the USA in February, but she wasn't among the lucky recipients. "We're happy as children to hear from you, and will continue to hope and bear up patiently until this difficult time is passed and we have lived through it." But conditions continued to deteriorate. "I can't assure you that we are all well. Hunger plagues us and it's impossible to buy food since we don't have ration cards." Even the funds my grandparents received from Switzerland were only of little help. "If we must be here much longer, eating will be catastrophically difficult, since one can buy almost nothing, even with a lot of money."

Meanwhile, my Dreifuss Opa fared even worse. For someone who was attached to familiar surroundings and people he knew, being uprooted three times within a year – first from his home in October 1940, then from Gurs in the spring of 1941, and finally from Noe in the fall of that year for internment in Recebedou – must have been a dreadful burden and quite bewildering. He could not survive in such strange surroundings for very long and died December 19, 1941. Oma told us the news in a letter that failed to reach us; she reiterated it in a second letter sent from Marseilles in early January 1942: "Sadly, dear father Ludwig died in Recebedou." The news was confirmed in a brief note from HIAS in early February, apparently the result of an inquiry from my father.

The winter of 1941-42 must have been especially hard for my Oma and Opa. They were able to see each other regularly, but not as often or for as long a time as they would have wished. Les Milles was an hour's walk from Marseilles, an arduous trip in the cold months. In addition, Opa had a flare up of kidney stones that had been diagnosed several years earlier, but only treated with medication. Fortunately, he was able to get medical help in Aix and was able to buy the necessary medicines. In the process, he used most of the funds that had been sent to them for food and daily living expenses. "The end result is that, thank God, the stone passed." Oma wrote, "You can imagine that this also lifted a stone from our hearts."

Daddy continued his efforts to obtain the needed documents for Oma and Opa to immigrate to the United States. This was especially difficult since the rules kept shifting. In February 1942, he was informed by the State Department that "developments incidental to the war have made it necessary to reexamine certain aspects of this case (the visa of my grandparents)". Three weeks later, HIAS informed him that persons in unoccupied France might be able to pay their own passage if they can get the francs and have them converted into dollars. Daddy turned to the AFSC for help, and they advised him they had channels to their office in Marseilles through London, so send money to London! But without visa authorization, no action was possible, so this avenue was put on hold.

The summer brought a bit of relief from the biting cold of the winter, and with it came a bit of hope as well. The American consulate issued authorizations for emigration with some regularity, although still at much too slow a pace, and never for Oma and Opa. The lack of authorization was particularly painful for them since only those with appointments at the consulate were allowed leave from Les Milles. Thus, Opa was unable to come to Marseilles for many weeks. The regular stream of letters in the spring and early summer of 1942 were full of gossip about relatives and friends, about the urgency for funds, about the longing for an end to the war. In late May, Oma wrote, "The main thing is that we, thank God, are satisfied with our health, although you probably wouldn't recognize me any more since I've lost so much weight . . . but there's no point in being upset, we simply have to endure." "Just now, the weather is already quite warm, with cool evenings and mornings. The nature is quite beautiful, though we take no pleasure in it; only faith in God helps us to keep up our hope."

During the spring of 1942, more and more internees were shipped out of Gurs to the other camps in France and, of course, East. Oma indicates that the hotel was getting more and more crowded, with women in every possible space. Often, the new arrivals were acquaintances from Gurs and brought with them news of still others. With so many newcomers, food became scarcer than ever and also much more expensive. To stretch their meager funds, Oma tried to work as often as possible in the kitchen. "Then I receive a double ration of soup and somewhat more Lechem (bread), all on the q.t. I try to send some of the bread to dear Sigmund, so that we can save a bit since it's enormously expensive to buy anything."

An indication of the systematic depopulation of the camps and the planned closing of Gurs came in a letter dated August 17:

> *"Unfortunately, I have to share with you now the news that on the 12 of August 1942, dear Siegfried (Elsie's father), along with hundreds of men and women, was transported from here to a destination unknown. You have probably heard about it already via radio and news reports. I'll desist from describing the scene for you, we've had so much of this that we need to quiet our nerves. We can only hope that dear Siegfried will have a lucky fate and get sent back. I don't know more; the terrible situation is so frightful."*

The fall of 1942 was full of hope and despair. Daddy received a letter from the State Department indicating that advisory approval had been granted for immigration visas for Sigmund and Anna Valfer. The office in Marseilles was being notified. He was also informed that "The American Consul will withhold a visa from any applicant who fails to produce proof of overseas transportation." Daddy acted immediately. He contacted HIAS and sent them the funds necessary to pay for ship's passage: $1040 for the two tickets plus $3.50 to cover cable charges. The $520 charge per person was quite an increase from the $111 we had had to pay just three years earlier. The total amount was more than the cash we had available, so Elsie transferred funds originally set aside for the passage of her father, Siegfried. By October 29, all the funds were in place and only final authorization for immigration to the US was needed.

Meanwhile, Opa had been sent to Nexon, an internment camp near Limoges that imprisoned mainly Jews over age 60. The change was very difficult since it meant that my grandparents could no longer see each other (Nexon was over 100 km. from Marseilles). Still, some hope remained, especially after Oma received communications from the American consulate that her case was being reviewed. "Still, there is no Visa de Sorti, and we hope that it will yet arrive. In any case, this connection provides me with some advantages and has a calming effect."

The approval from the State Department and the payment of funds came too late. The authorization could never be issued. On November 7, 1942 Allied troops invaded North Africa for a first direct encounter with Hitler's army. The Vichy government was immediately suspended and the Nazis occupied all of France. All borders were closed. Emigration through official channels became impossible. Only trickles of mail, very sporadic, still kept connections alive.

Within a week of the invasion, Jews living in the transit hotels in Marseilles were being transferred elsewhere. Oma was sent to Nexon, which meant a grateful reunion with Opa. Her letter of November 21 indicates, "We are very glad to be together, no matter what happens; we can see and speak with each other every day, and each can help the other. If only dear God would also help. I would not have thought that we'd have to go back into a camp, but what can we do." Stoically, Oma was grateful for continued good health. Her letter is full of news about relatives, concern that they hadn't heard from Siegfried (did they really not know about the death camps?), recognition of the High Holy Days and of family birthdays, and great delight in the news about our activities in America, especially my own progress in school.

It was the last letter we received from them. Airmail that had taken 4 to 6 weeks in either direction now took even longer. In desperation for word of my grandparents' welfare, my parents turned to the Red Cross for help. A message was sent in January 1943; three months later, the return was delivered, with yet another address: Camp de Masseube. Apparently, the Jews still remaining in southern France were being shunted from place to place, especially after Gurs was closed in November 1943. But the reply held some reassurance: "Lines gladden us. Both well. Faller takes care of us. We hear nothing from Mayer. Hugs, kisses, especially Alice and Ilse."

My parents sent a second message via the Red Cross in September, which elicited a reply in February 1944. The reply was similar to the earlier message, but again, the address had changed, this time to Hotel Beau Seyour, Alboussiere, Ardeche. Regularly in 1943 and sporadically until mid-April 1944, Oma and Opa continued to be sent mail from Alfred Faller, both francs and small packages. How much of this they actually received is not known. For us, the last communication came from the Hotel Beau Seyour. Within a month, Oma and Opa were shipped to Drancy (a transit camp close to Paris, used as a gathering point for further transport to camps in the East), and from there, on April 7, 1944 made their final journey by cattle car to Auschwitz. Official records put the date of death as December 31, 1944, but it is doubtful that they survived even the initial selection on their arrival in Auschwitz. Most likely, they were sent immediately to the gas chambers where they were turned into smoke and ashes.

May their memory be for a blessing.

Making a Place of Our Own

We moved to New London with only a few household items that Janet Johl had given us as she was closing up the house at Trails Corner – a few old pots and pans, a very mismatched set of cutlery and dishes, a few old sheets. Since we had no savings, and therefore no funds with which to buy furniture, we rented a furnished apartment located at 28 Linden St. Once again, we were on the third floor, but, unlike our other third floor living quarters, this one was reached only by the back stairs and had no access to the floors below it.

The apartment had two bedrooms, a large front living room, and a large but ill equipped kitchen, with a coal-burning stove which served both for cooking and for heat, a sink without cabinet, one cupboard, and a large round table and chairs. Our food was kept cold in an icebox tucked into a corner of the kitchen. Every few days, we put a sign in our window for the iceman, who would notice whether the sign read $0.25 or $0.35, and deliver the appropriate sized block of ice to our door. It became my chore to empty the pan in which the water collected under the icebox as the ice melted. Most of the time, this was no problem, but occasionally I forgot. Whenever that happened, I was reminded by the forceful knock of a broom handle on the ceiling of the apartment below us. I always wondered what their ceiling looked like, with its many water stains and bangs from the broom handle.

Once again, I had to deal with a new school. My parents initially enrolled me in Harbor School, which serviced the "better" part of town.

Students there included many of the children I had met at Hebrew school. But after two weeks, the School Department determined that an error had been made in my school assignment. We lived on the north side of Willetts Avenue, which was the dividing line for two school districts. I was reassigned to Nameaug School, some six blocks from our apartment. Fifth grade at Nameaug was a lively class, with many activities and a diverse group of youngsters. Naturally, I was the object of some curiosity when I first appeared, but gradually was accepted by the class, and I settled in. My fifth school in just over two years, my enrollment at Nameaug finally marked the beginning of my orderly progression through a school system.

Daddy had a long commute to his work as a night watchman in the plant in Groton. This involved changing buses and carefully watching his time, since he had to travel in the late afternoon and again in very early morning. Occasionally, Mama and I took the bus to visit with him in the evening, bringing supper along so that we could eat as a family. Mama looked for work as soon as we were settled. She found a job at Weintraub's Clothing Factory, a sweat shop making children's dresses in a second floor loft, located just next to Nameaug School. Most of the workers were Italian women, the majority named Mary. To distinguish them, they were called Buttonhole Mary, Seam Mary, etc. Mama was assigned to putting sleeves on the dresses, not an ideal job, but the income was essential. She was a conscientious worker and had no trouble being accepted by the other workers.

This must have been a very difficult period for my parents who were on such different schedules and had almost none of the comforts that make life pleasant. Nor could their work have been a source of satisfaction for them. Their lives were determined by the work schedule, giving them even less flexibility than their previous positions as household help. Nor did the jobs provide any kind of stimulation for them, either in terms of the use of their minds or their skills in the business world. And a constant in their lives was concern for family in Europe, although the entrance of the United States into the war in December 1941 gave some slight hope of an early end to the fighting. Somehow, despite all the hardships and worry, both managed to remain optimistic. Daddy's sense of humor never left him, their faith that all would end well remained steadfast, and their love of each other and of me created a home that was warm and cheerful. I never felt deprived or poor.

Summer vacations posed a challenge for my working parents. During the summer of 1942, I was enrolled in a city program that met at a small beach on Pequot Avenue. The beach itself was more stone and debris than sand, but my daily time there afforded me a chance to swim and I enjoyed the activities at the small park across the street. The following summer was filled with anxiety about polio. Any sneeze or sign of a cold was interpreted as the onset of the dread disease. Ocean water was considered dangerous. So another summer at the Pequot Ave. beach was ruled out. Instead, my parents purchased a season's pass for me to Ocean Beach and its pool. It was thought that the pool was a safer environment. I went almost daily to the pool, where I loved being able to use the diving board, and also to roam the boardwalk and meet people I knew. Most of the time, I traveled the three miles by bus, but occasionally, I met Henry Linz (son of my parents' friends) and we walked the three miles to and from the beach.

New London had a relatively small Jewish community, mostly constituted of Jews whose origins were in Eastern Europe. By the time we arrived, however, several German Jewish refugees had gravitated there. We were soon part of that circle – a group of families who had left things German behind, but who still felt more comfortable among folks with similar backgrounds. The children all went to Temple Beth El's Hebrew school and Shabbat morning junior congregation, and the parents met socially on occasion. Still, many years passed before any of the adults ventured to address one another by first name; it was Mr. Linz, Mrs. Bernstein, Mr. Liebenau. The group was expanded with the arrival of several single refugee men, and these found a welcome home in our apartment on Linden Street.

The presence of single men allowed Mama to augment our income by offering them regular meals for a fee. Several joined us for the evening meal, but one also came for lunch, which Mama prepared and put in the ice box, and which I then had to put on the table as soon as I came home from school just after noon. The men were happy to take advantage of such an arrangement since they had no real homes of their own. The one who remained with us the longest was Ralph Sanford. A highly regarded lawyer in Berlin, he fled to New London, where he worked as a janitor in a moving company warehouse. His long-term goal was to study American law and regain his status as a lawyer, which he did many years later. Meanwhile, he continued his habit of being a fastidious dresser, very conscious of his carefully slicked back black hair and highly polished shoes. Much to my chagrin, he became a fixture in our apartment, especially on Sunday evenings. We had purchased a radio (essential for getting the latest war news), and it was Ralph Sanford's habit of always listening to WQXR, the classical music station. This meant I was deprived of "Ozzie and Harriet", "The Jack Benny Show", and "Allen's Alley" whenever he was around. On the bright side, he was also responsible for my getting out of school earlier than others on snow days. Typically, we were dismissed on those days shortly after 1:00 PM, but I had to walk home promptly at noon (our usual lunch hour) in order to get his lunch on the table.

One of the first major items that we bought once we were settled in New London was a used car. It was a huge help for Daddy, who no longer had to depend on bus schedules, but it also reflected his love of cars and of driving. The war necessitated strict gas rationing, and our driving needs were clearly nonessential – we were issued a "D ration" sticker. This didn't allow us to buy enough gasoline to permit any regular use of the car, so we sold it within a couple of years.

Among our friends were the Mayers, refugees from the area near Kenzingen. They had been resettled on a farm in Lebanon, CT, where they could continue their work with cattle. Their farm was a pleasant destination for a Sunday drive, while we still had our car, and we often returned home with a freshly slaughtered chicken from their barnyard. It also served as the gathering place for New London's German Jews at Pesach. The Mayers' house was large enough to accommodate all of us around their table for a communal *seder*. My strongest memories of those celebrations center on a long service, followed by a longer meal, after which all of us children crept out of the room to fall asleep under the coats piled on the bed in an adjoining room.

Fortunately, by the time we sold our car, it was no longer such a necessity. Daddy had left his job as night watchman and accepted a position in New London as night warehouseman for the Montgomery Ward department store. Although this was still a night job, it meant much less commuting time. Daddy was delighted to be back in a merchandising milieu, and worked hard to organize the warehouse efficiently. In several months, he was promoted to warehouse manager, a daytime work schedule, and a raise in pay. One of the great advantages of his new position was his access to damaged merchandise. He used his spare time to refinish/repair the items that he considered useful, which he was then free to take home. We gradually acquired our own bedroom furniture, living room pieces, and kitchen cabinets.

The first two years in New London were very frugal ones for us. Salaries were very low (the family income for 1942 was $1258, raised to $1970 in 1943), and we sent every spare penny to grandparents stranded in France. Fortunately, we enjoyed eating the cheaper cuts of meat, like lung, spleen, heart, and liver, which Mama bought from the kosher butcher (though we didn't keep kosher). New clothes were rare, though I grew enough to warrant an annual change of wardrobe. Mama was able to get some of my dresses at Weinberg's factory, where the help could buy items at below-wholesale cost. Elsie also supplied clothes, not always to my liking, which she bought at discount in New York. I particularly remember a winter jacket – a navy blue, heavy wool pea jacket that I had to wear even though all the other girls had long wool coats with hoods. I compensated by imagining the clothes I'd really like and drawing them for a set of paper dolls that were among my favorite toys.

One area in which Mama splurged was books. She regularly bought books to supplement the ones we borrowed from the library. I soon had a substantial collection – all of Louisa May Alcott, translations of old favorites ("Nobody's Boy," Grimm and Andersen fairy tales), "Little Lord Fauntleroy," the Bobbsey Twins, and Nancy Drew. I read constantly, and became familiar with Norse mythology and German folklore, as well as the Wizard of Oz. I also read reams of comic books -- at night, under the covers -- passed along to me by Henry Linz. On one occasion, Mama bought me a book of opera stories, complete with bars of music and lovely illustrations. Saturday afternoons soon became devoted to listening to live broadcasts from the Metropolitan Opera, with the opera book propped open before me at the kitchen table.

I led a fairly lonely existence in these years (although it's only in retrospect that I recognize it as such). In part, I was reluctant to make friends who might desert me just as my German friends had deserted me in Kenzingen. In part, my interests were somewhat different from most of my schoolmates – they were hardly likely to want to listen to opera or read at the ferocious pace that was normal for me. I was also too poor to spend money on things like movies, which, even at $0.25 a ticket, were only very occasional treats. And finally, my parents continued to be extremely protective of me, a pattern that had been established well before we left Germany. As a result, I seldom played in the street, and it was several years before I was allowed to walk to the center of town by myself or with friends.

Because we had our own very personal stake in the fate of the Nazis, we intensely followed the military news via newspaper and radio. We subscribed to the *New London Day*, but also to *PM* and the Sunday *New York Times*. I felt cheated because the *Times* carried no comics, but I appreciated the political cartoons in *PM* and its strong anti-Nazi stand. I was always gratified to learn that the Nazis faced opposition, though it was some time before they were actually beaten in battle. We also subscribed to *Aufbau*, a newspaper for the German Jewish community in the United States that carried special reports on events involving German Jews, and that was instrumental in reuniting families after the war. Daddy was pleased to be able to do the crossword puzzle in German in the *Aufbau*, and later also the one in the Sunday *Times* in English.

We were always conscious of the war and were made aware of it in many strange ways. Since we were ostensibly of German nationality, we were classified as "enemy aliens," and had to register annually at the post office, so that our whereabouts was tracked. Twice a year, we were visited by FBI agents, who searched our apartment for hidden short-wave radios and firearms. Such a farcical use of personnel! Our reaction was to be as patriotic as possible, carefully saving all scraps of metal and pressing all our tin cans flat so they could be donated to the many scrap metal drives. Nameaug School placed a large dumpster in front of the school for collection of such scrap. My greatest pleasure was to throw into it the Iron Cross decoration that Daddy had carefully preserved as proof of his service in the German Army in World War I. I hoped that it would be turned into a bullet and find an appropriate mark. Daddy also registered with the draft once it was instituted, but was classified "4F" because of an irregular heart beat.

New London was considered a strategic location because of its nearby submarine base and Electric Boat, a key plant for producing subs. Thus special precautions were taken to prepare the residents for possible attack. Windows had to have light-proof black coverings, and car headlights were taped half way to reduce light from the beams. In school, we practiced air raids, and the girls learned skills that might prepare them to serve as nurses' aides. We were taught how to make beds with hospital corners (I still do it that way), how to move patients to prevent bed sores, how to care for infants.

We became members of Temple Beth El as soon as we were settled in New London, so that I could continue my Hebrew education. Since Mama and Daddy both worked on Saturdays (a half day for Mama), they were not able to attend services regularly, but attended as often as possible. Mama always maintained that attending and participating in responsive readings was a great way to improve one's English pronunciation. Who would have known, for example, that "interpret" was accented on the middle syllable and not on the first, like "interview" or "interlude"?

I went to junior congregation regularly, as well as to Hebrew school twice during the week and on Sundays. I stayed out of school for all the holidays, when children's services were available. The walks to and from services helped to strengthen my friendship with Adele Diamond, who lived near us and also attended Beth El. Often, on our walks home we had the company of Rabbi Meyer Kripke, who lived even further away from the synagogue than we did.

The High Holy Days were particularly difficult for Mama and Daddy, since they brought back the many memories of the happy celebrations with grandparents in Freiburg. Inevitably, one of the rabbi's sermons dealt with the catastrophe in Europe and often gave rich detail of the atrocities being committed by the Nazis. Mama sat through them with tears coursing down her cheeks. Clearly, by 1942 and 1943, the word had spread about what was happening in Europe and about the realities of the death camps. For us personally, it was agonizing not to know what was happening to Mama's parents, who were interned in France, or to Daddy's three brothers still in Europe.

By the fall of 1943, we had accumulated enough household items and some savings to enable us to move into an unfurnished apartment in a two-family house. Its location was hardly an improvement of neighborhood. Belden Street was a dead end street in a decidedly working class area. Our landlord was an Italian family – the Barcas -- who delighted in their vegetable and flower garden, but whose cooking odors (olive oil, garlic, and melted cheese) were more than Daddy could bear. We kept our doors tightly closed. Our neighbor was a Jewish junk dealer who parked his horse and buggy outside his house. A vacant, overgrown lot and a muddy brook marked the end of the street, next to the house in which we lived.

The apartment itself had a front porch and front entrance as well as a side door, two bedrooms, a large eat-in kitchen, living room, and bathroom. We essentially lived in the kitchen, where the oil stove/range provided heat for the entire space. The living room was barely used and usually kept closed off, an echo of the formal parlor in our apartment in Kenzingen. I had a small desk in my room, but normally spent my time at the kitchen table, absorbed in my books, hardly aware of others around me. For me, an advantage of the new apartment was its greater proximity to Jennings School, the middle school where I now attended 7th and 8th grade. We no longer had boarders for whom I had to prepare lunch, but I still walked home most days for the hour-long lunch break.

After my experiences in Germany with the untrustworthiness of friends, I was reluctant to reach out in friendship to most people and always kept a slight barrier around myself. But by the time I was in seventh grade, I had begun to develop some friendships with girls who were in my classes and who also went to Hebrew School with me. My closest friend, Adele Diamond, shared my unusual interest in classical music because she was studying the violin. She also came from a family who had to watch their expenditures carefully, and, like me, couldn't easily indulge in some of the activities that other girls in our class enjoyed. Interest in boys for both of us was for the distant future, though I did try – in vain – to interest one of the boys in my class, Herman Goldstein, in being my partner in the dance classes that were part of our middle school gym program.

I always remained something of an outsider. First, I was a refugee; second I came from Germany, and German Jews were not considered "real" Jews by the East European Jewish community. I knew nothing about bagels, latkes (potato pancakes), lukshen kugel (noodle pudding), or borsht (beet soup). How could I possibly be an authentic Jew? I compensated by losing myself in books and school work – which also served to create a distance between me and others. In striving so hard in school, I was unconsciously fulfilling my parents' expectations: I had to succeed because I was the only offspring on both sides of the family and therefore had to do well. Fortunately, school work came easily so the burden was more sub-conscious than overt. But it did set me apart from others. Still, "being good" in all kinds of ways, including being an obedient daughter, was a theme running throughout my life.

When I was in seventh grade, Mama developed carpal tunnel syndrome and had to leave her job at Weinberg's Dress Factory. To augment Daddy's wages, she turned to an area she knew and enjoyed – cooking. She began to build up a small private catering business, doing mostly cocktail parties and home events. Then she took a great risk, and rented space in a building on Bank Street, only a few blocks from our home, to open a fine candy store – "La Bonbonierre". The store featured fine European candies (Bartons and Barraccini), but also sold pastries that Mama baked in the large space in back of the retail area. It also served as a staging ground for the parties Mama continued to cater. But the timing for such a store was poor and the location not good. Sugar continued to be rationed throughout the war, so that candies and the supplies for baking were limited. The kind of clientele Mama hoped to attract was also unlikely to come to the area where the store was located– away from the central business district. Her most regular clients were the children from Nameaug School just across the street, for whom she had put in a supply of penny candy.

The store lasted just two years, but it was there, on April 15, 1945 that we learned of the death of President Franklin Delano Roosevelt and, a few weeks later, on May 8, of the surrender of the German forces and the end of the war in Europe. We celebrated like everyone around us, and with prayers for speedy news about our loved ones still in Europe. Our future was firmly set in America, but it was difficult to shake off the past.

Accountings

Once the war in Europe had ended, our thoughts immediately turned to learning what had happened to those left behind, Oma and Opa and Daddy's three brothers, Julius, Max, and Adolf.

Of most urgency was to trace Oma and Opa, from whom we'd had no word for over a year, since February of 1944. Alfred Faller, who had been so helpful and had sent funds to Oma and Opa as long as possible, wrote immediately after the war to indicate that he had no news about their whereabouts, and could only hope for a miracle. Mama and Daddy didn't give up. They carefully read lists of survivors' names published in *Aufbau* (the German-Jewish-American newspaper) and by the UN Relief and Rehabilitation Agency. Among the lists of survivors of Terezin (Theresienstadt) was one Anna Valter. Mama contacted the Red Cross; could the name perhaps be Anna Valfer? In August, a telegram from the Red Cross indicated, "Anna Valter not mother of Greta Dreifuss." The search continued until we finally received notification from the Red Cross that Oma and Opa had been deported to Auschwitz in the spring of 1944, and that their date of death was officially set as December 1944.

Aufbau was helpful in other ways. Not only did it list names of survivors, it also carried ads of persons in the United States seeking loved ones in Europe. An ad that Daddy had placed brought results. We received a note from Uncle Julius, who, with Meta, was still living in Germany! Julius and Meta had been able to continue living in their home in Duesseldorf for some time after the war began. Julius was active in maintaining the Jewish community, which held services until well into 1942. At mid-year, the deportations from Duesseldorf began. Julius spent time in a number of concentration camps, including Buchenwald, where he had also been interred in 1938 after *Kristallnacht*. Just before the camps were liberated, Julius somehow managed to escape and go into hiding, thanks to a courageous neighbor in Duesseldorf who provided shelter in his cellar. What a risk that must have been! Meta, who was a convert to Judaism, was spared the deportations and spent the war in the city. She and Julius were reunited after the fall of the Nazis.

Aunt Meta and Uncle Julius Dreifuss, Stuttgart, Germany, 1950

At that point, Julius swore that he would remain living in Germany because he would not be party to giving Hitler the final victory of making Germany *Judenrein* (clean of Jews). Instead, Julius and Meta worked for the rest of their lives to rebuild the Jewish community of the northern Rhine region. In September 1945, Julius led the very first Rosh Hashanah service in Duesseldorf since liberation. He subsequently was elected president of the northern Rhine community, became a member of the Executive Committee of Freed Jews in the British Zone, and eventually served on the Directorate of the Central Council of German Jews. Both he and Meta helped provide a safe haven for Jews, especially the children who came to live in the area, and were strong supporters of Israel. But, despite their resolve to continue living and working in Germany, being surrounded by so many memories of the Nazi past was anathema to them both. They compensated by buying a small house in Holland, just over the border from Duesseldorf, where they went for respite as often as possible. Julius and my father never saw each other again.

Uncle Max and Aunt Gretel also survived the war inside Germany. They were living in Berlin when the Nazis came to power. Max was involved in selling opticals and Gretel was a secretary. Because Max looked so much like his mother – blond and blue-eyed, he could easily pass as an Aryan. Jews were issued yellow stars some time after the war began, but Max seldom wore his. Together with some false identification papers, he was able to live a relatively normal life. He had one more source of protection. Like Meta, Gretel was born a non-Jew (though, also like Meta, she had converted to Judaism), and the Nazis debated for several years about how to handle mixed marriages. Husbands in such marriages (intermarriages at that time were much less likely to involved a Jewish wife and non-Jewish husband) were not initially subjected to the deportations like their fellow Jews.

Uncle Max and Aunt Gretel Dreifuss, Berlin, 1937

However, once the Nazis had decided on the Final Solution, even these men were at risk. To avoid alarming their wives, the men were assembled in early 1943 at a Jewish welfare office on Rosenstrasse, awaiting reassignment (ostensibly) to work camps. At that point, the Aryan women in Berlin who were married to Jewish men, and the women's families, understood what was happening and began a protest! Without organization or leadership, they marched, in small groups and then in large groups numbering in the hundreds, to the Reichstag to demand that their husbands not be deported. What courage! It's hard to imagine Aunt Gretel, the meekest of women, being involved in such a daring enterprise. Yet, by participating in the Rosenstrasse Protest, she helped to save her husband. Amazingly, the Nazis backed off and indicated that the men would simply be assigned to a special corps to assist in civil defense. They were ordered to clean out buildings and douse fires after Allied bombing raids. The raids were frequent and intense, and the work was extremely dangerous, but somehow Max survived.

At war's end, Max and Gretel were assigned to a displaced persons camp in Frankfurt, operated by the American Joint Distribution Committee. That they were assigned to Frankfurt was probably no coincidence, since Gretel had some family in the area. Through UNRRA (United Nations Relief and Rehabilitation Agency) Max was able to locate his brother – Daddy – in New London. Imagine our pleasure when we received a small folded card from them: "We are healthy, await news from you soon. A more detailed letter is on its way. Warmest greetings and kisses, Max and Gretel."

Max was determined to leave Germany behind him as soon as possible. He and Gretel (they had no children) applied for visas to the United States, with Daddy as sponsor. Since Daddy by then was earning the great sum of $2340 a year, he was able to guarantee their welfare upon arrival. They sailed into New York in 1945 and began to follow a trajectory much like that of Mama and Daddy. They took a position as household help with a family in Groton, CT, close enough to our home so that they could be with us on their days off. It enabled them to begin learning English and to save some funds. After two years, Max found a good job in retail work in Louisville, KY, where, soon after, he unfortunately developed cancer. He is buried in Louisville.

After his death, Gretel came to live with us in New London, but was extremely homesick for her family in Germany. By 1950, she decided to move back to Germany, where she was eligible for a good pension and had family support.

Of the three brothers, Uncle Adolf was the one who remained in touch the longest. He had fled Germany precipitously for France in 1937 because of his outspoken opposition to the Nazis. France, however, was not eager to support Jewish refugees, and provided scant opportunities for work. The one avenue most open was the Foreign Legion, a French military unit that was created to solve the employment problem for unwanted residents – criminals, homeless, refugees. Adolf joined the Foreign Legion in 1939 and was sent to North Africa. Once the Nazis overran France, they also took over the Foreign Legion; Adolf, like the entire unit, found himself impressed into service by Rommel (the German commander of North Africa), helping to build a railroad across the desert. His letters from that time described the intense daytime heat and freezing nights. We sent him scarves, gloves and salamis; he received empty boxes. Eventually his letters stopped altogether.

Uncle Adolf Dreifuss in uniform of Free French Army, with friend, 1944

When the Allies landed in North Africa and began a victorious sweep of the territory, the Foreign Legion reverted to French control and became an arm of the Free French Army under Gen. Charles de Gaulle. He resumed contact with us and sent us a picture of himself, looking fit and pleased in the uniform of a French soldier. Adolf, as a member of the now Free French Army, helped in the liberation of France and was present at the triumphant entry of the Allies into Paris. He stayed in Paris, married a French widow, and established a furniture store in the Marche aux Puces. In 1963, he and his wife made a grand tour of the United States and spent two weeks with Daddy, exploring New England.

The stories of my father's three brothers illustrate how varied the trajectories for survival were. Individual personalities, differing circumstance, and luck all played a role. That all three survived at all is amazing. Their decisions on how to spend the remainder of their lives also took three distinct paths. The only commonality is that none of them had children, which may have been a decisive factor in both their survival and their post-war lives.

Within a year of the end of the war in Europe, we knew the fates of our closest relatives. We also knew that many of Mama's uncles, aunts, and cousins had survived as well. They had managed to escape from Europe and reached the United States at various times, some via Switzerland, some via Cuba, some via Latin America. Our happiest surprise had been to encounter quite by chance Mama's cousin Hanna on the streets of New York in July 1941, while we spent our week's vacation in the city. Even more surprising, Hanna had a tiny daughter, Suzie, with her.

By 1946, then, many of the concerns for family had been resolved. While we continued to mourn the deaths of my two sets of grandparents, we recognized how fortunate we were to have had most of our immediate family survive the war period. We were ready to look ahead and establish our lives firmly in America. Like Americans everywhere, there was ground for optimism. Daddy had found work that suited his skills. Mama learned how to parlay her expertise with food into a modest business. I was moving along in school, doing well, and meeting the high expectations of my parents. We applied for citizenship, certain that we had found a place where we could live in peace.

Faith, Love, and Echoes

Over two centuries, the story of my family has been one of modest beginnings, adjustments, and continuity despite change. Since my ancestors settled in the mid-18th century in southwest Germany, they have found for themselves niches in the local economy, social ties both within and outside their religious community, maintenance of traditions even while adapting to local ways, and a strong sense of who they were as human beings and as Jews. As members of a minority religion, they must to some extent have always felt different, yet they were able to make themselves at home in settings as varied as villages and large cities, rural Germany and urban America. Their inner sense of identity was surely critical to their survival.

I am overwhelmed by the ability of my parents to begin new lives in the United States without bitterness or hate, and to remain optimists when events demanded pessimism. How difficult it must have been for them to assume the roles of domestic servants after having the independence and status that business ownership conferred. Yet, they carried out their duties with dignity and strove to do the best they could. Having the safety of America, shelter and food guaranteed, and some discretionary funds to send to family trapped in Germany must have served as some consolation for their low status.

Although they never again wanted to have anything to do with Germany and Germans, and they regarded any Germans they met with an unspoken, skeptical "What were you doing during the war?"

they did not let this attitude prevent them from leading fulfilling lives. They blended the best of their past with their hope for the future. They continued to appreciate the cultural heritage of Germany, and made classical music the standard in our home. At the same time, they also kept up with local popular music and could always name the top tunes on the musical hit parade. My father transformed his involvement with soccer into a devotion to baseball; as an ardent Yankee fan, he was able to cite all the team statistics. My mother continued her love of literature by joining the Book of the Month Club and becoming a regular user of the local library. Although they spoke with a German accent, English was the common language at home, with only an occasional German phrase creeping in. My father became as adept at doing crossword puzzles in English as he had been in German.

Our early years in the United States were economically constrained, yet I seldom felt poor or deprived. We always ate nutritious meals. Mama cooked a combination of traditional European foods and inexpensive versions of the dishes she had learned to make while working for American families in Vermont and Connecticut. Her experiences in making do after the Nazi boycott had cut off our source of livelihood was good training for our first years in New London, when our low income and wartime rationing of meat, sugar, and coffee dictated our diet.

Mama often maintained that the major lesson she learned from the Nazi period was the unimportance of things and the great value of people. She had greatly prized all the crystal, silver, and china that had been part of her household. Once they were gone, she had few regrets, even as she continued to appreciate quality goods. That so many of her relatives had been murdered or dispersed never ceased to cause pain. She, and Daddy, translated these feelings into a desire to help others. No solicitor for a good cause was turned away from our door, and, when possible, my parents volunteered for charitable organizations. They became strong Zionists, because they recognized the importance of creating a haven for Jews in a world that had refused them succor at a critical time.

My parents' devotion to Judaism never wavered. As domestic servants in largely secular homes, they could not observe the laws of *kashrut* or Shabbat, but they observed the holidays as much as possible. Once they had a home of their own, they tried to include more observance, although they continued to have to work on Saturdays and did not have the means to keep *kosher*. Nonetheless, Shabbat became a special time, and we joined a synagogue and attended services as regularly as possible. My parents made sure I received a religious education and attended services even when they could not. I was kept out of school on the Jewish holidays in order to participate in religious observances.

We joined Temple Beth El, the Conservative synagogue of New London. This provided us with a modest sense of community, although we never truly felt we "belonged." We were German Jews amid a congregation of East European origin; we were poor among people who were generally quite well to do. But Judaism and faith in God were integral parts of our lives, just as they had been for my grandparents, who never gave up that faith, even in the concentration camps.

Most of all, my parents devoted themselves to making me feel loved and to protecting me from anything they saw as frightening. This meant that they never discussed my grandparents' plight in front of me, never talked to me about their traumas under Nazi rule, never expressed their frustrations and doubts about their first years in America within my hearing. They even went so far as to shield me as much as possible from scary children's movies, even though I read and loved fairy tales full of witches and ogres.

At the same time, our difficult past reached into the present as I grew up. I sensed that I carried the burden of the future of the family. As the only grandchild on either side of the family, I became the focal point of all the hopes of my grandparents (quite clear in their letters from the camps) and was always under pressure from my parents to do well. This meant, first of all, being obedient to their wishes -- being "good;" it also meant knowing my place as the child of servants while we lived in Bennington and Groton. I was expected to do well in school, which, fortunately, was easy for me. My primary goal was to please my parents, and I felt guilty if I failed in any way.

This unspoken pressure had long-term repercussions. I was hesitant to speak out, both in school and among peers. I raised my hand only if I was sure I had the right answer, and found it difficult to speak in front of the class. I had difficulty making friends, for a number of reasons. At first, there was obviously a communication problem, compounded by my parents' demands that I go straight home after school. For two years, I had no home of my own to which I could invite potential friends, and so none could ask me back. Once we settled in New London, I did socialize with several of the other Jewish girls in my class, but never developed a close relation with any of them. I always felt "different," and additionally felt stigmatized by getting good grades.

But there was another underlying factor causing me to keep apart, one that stemmed from my experiences in Germany. There, I had many friends, almost all of whom deserted me in response to Nazi propaganda and laws. I learned at a very early age, that friends were not constant and could not be trusted. Even my school mates in the Jewish school in Freiburg, who were in similar positions to mine, did not become my friends. We all had similar experiences of desertion by our German friends, and had little opportunity or inclination in school to get to know each other. We were all brought to school and hurried home after school by our guardians. In fact, at a 60th reunion of fellow members of that school, none of us could remember the others; as Jewish children in Germany, we had learned not to make friends. That lesson stayed with me for a very long time; only in adulthood did I feel comfortable developing trust and true friendships.

My family's story is not unique. Tales of flight from persecution, and specifically flight from the Nazi terror, have been replicated many times over. My parents and I were extremely fortunate to have been able to duplicate the pattern of resettlement and acculturation in America that had characterized my ancestors moving from 18th century Alsace to Germany. At the same time, we continued to be outside the larger society just as those early Jewish migrants to Altdorf had been. For Jews, outsider status was never completely erased, of course, as the Nazis made abundantly clear. In America, being German, German-Jews, and refuges, in addition to being poor all added to our otherness. Moreover, for many years, no one in America seemed to care enough to listen to our history. And internally, we bore the burden of guilt for having survived when so many of our family had not.

Nonetheless, our lives in our new country have been satisfying and full of optimism, even while they were much more complex than would appear on the surface. My parents achieved a comfortable standard of living that allowed them the small luxuries of theater, concerts, and occasional vacation trips. Our Jewish identities became an amalgam of German, East European, and American traditions that allowed us to feel comfortable not only in our Conservative synagogue, but also in the community at large. My facility in school earned me a college education. Finally, my marriage resulted in the happy triumph of three children and seven grandchildren, all secure in being Jewish Americans.

Appendix

Family Foods

Most families treasure a series of recipes that are handed down from one generation to the next. Our family certainly had such traditions, some stemming from their origins in Alsace, others reflecting the cooking of southwest Germany and most specifically of the area around Kenzingen. Many of the foods are associated with Jewish holidays. Most of them traveled with us to the United States, where they were enjoyed, sometimes in modified form, by employers, friends, and family. Many are quite different from the foods that East European Jews brought with them, and that are generally considered "Jewish foods" in America. We knew nothing of bagels, latkes, or luxion kugel, but had our own specialties that we thought of as particularly Jewish. Alas, many are so artery clogging that they have become only fond memories on our taste buds.

Apple/Plum Compote

The festive Rosh Hashanah meal would not have been complete without an apple/plum compote. This tradition was carried over from Alsace, and takes advantage of seasonal produce. Since Mama would never have served a salad or pickles on Rosh Hashanah (in order to keep the new year sweet), the compote served as a very useful side dish to what was always a heavy meal.

6 large apples - Macintosh or Cortland work very well
2 lbs. Italian prune plums (about 12 plums)
1 Tbsp. cinnamon
½ c. sugar (optional)

Place all ingredients in large pot and add water to cover. Bring to boil, then simmer until apples and plums are tender. Refrigerate before using.

Chestnuts and Prunes

Because southern Germany was relatively close to Italy, a number of delicacies were imported and enjoyed by those of us living in the region. For me, the greatest treat was chestnuts. During the winter, vendors from Italy promoted roasted chestnuts (*heise Maroni)* on many street corners in Freiburg, and my Oma often stopped to buy me a small bag of them. At home, a favorite dessert was cooked chestnuts and prunes.

1 lb. fresh chestnuts
½ lb. pitted prunes
1/3 c. sugar
1 tsp. cinnamon
½ tsp. cloves
¼ tsp. salt
1/3 c. red wine
Water as needed

With a sharp knife, make two slits in each chestnut, then cover with water and boil until soft, about 45 minutes. While chestnuts are cooking, put prunes in bowl and cover with hot water.
Let chestnuts cool slightly in water, then remove one at a time and peel both the hard outer shell and the soft inner skin. When all chestnuts are peeled, put them and the prunes into a pot; reserve the water from the prunes. Add spices, sugar, and salt, then wine and enough of reserved water to cover. Simmer for up to one hour. Serve hot.

Creamy Spinach

This family favorite made its appearance during the Pesach holiday, when fresh spinach was readily available. That is why the recipe calls for the use of matzoh meal, since bread crumbs are prohibited during the holiday, but they can be used just as effectively as matzoh meal. I've always been surprised by the relatively sophisticated inclusion of ginger in the recipe. It's best to use fresh spinach for its intense flavor, but frozen spinach is also acceptable.

12 oz. fresh spinach, carefully washed and stripped of stems and woody spines.
1 small onion, finely diced
1 Tbsp. vegetable oil
½ tsp. powdered ginger
½ tsp. salt
½ tsp. garlic powder
½ c. matzoh meal or bread crumbs
Salt and pepper to taste

Steam the cleaned spinach in a small amount of water; it will reduce greatly in bulk. Drain spinach but reserve liquid. Chop spinach coarsely. Saute onion in oil until golden brown. Add spinach to onions and continue to sauté until some of the liquid from the spinach has evaporated. Remove from heat, add ginger, salt and pepper, matzoh meal, and some of the reserved liquid. Stir well. The spinach should be quite liquid; it will become firmer as it stands and absorbs the liquid and matzoh meal. Before serving, consistency can be adjusted by adding either more matzoh meal or more liquid. Heat carefully over low heat so that it does not stick to the bottom of the pan.

Goetterspeise

Goetterspeise translates as "Food for the Gods," and we considered it the very best dessert of all. It consists of four parts: sponge cake, peaches, wine sauce, and meringue. Since it takes some effort to make, it appeared very seldom at the table. And because it uses rather costly ingredients, Mama never made it the last few years we lived in Germany or for the first few years that we lived in New London. But it was a favorite in the Werblow and Johl households.

<u>Sponge cake</u>

4 eggs, separated
1 c. sugar
1 c. flour
1 tsp. baking powder
1/2 tsp. salt
¼ c. orange juice
½ tsp. vanilla

Beat egg whites until stiff. Set aside.
Beat sugar and egg yolks until lemon yellow. Add vanilla. Mix together dry ingredients and all alternately with the orange juice. Fold in beaten egg whites. Bake in well oiled loaf pan at 325 for 1 hour. Remove from pan and cool.

<u>Wine Sauce</u>

3 Tbsp. corn starch
4 Tbsp. sugar
4 eggs, beaten
1½ c. semi dry white wine
1 ½ c. water.
Mix dry ingredients. Slowly add eggs, then other liquids. Cook over double boiler till thick. Stir constantly and be sure the mixture doesn't come to a boil. Remove from heat and cool.

Meringue

3 egg whites
Pinch salt
1 Tbsp. sugar

Beat egg white until stiff. Slowly add salt and sugar and continue beating until very stiff.

To assemble, place slices of sponge cake at bottom and around sides of a serving dish. Layer with very ripe peaches (or canned peaches if fresh ones are not available). Cover with wine sauce. Repeat for another layer. Cover with meringue, being sure that the meringue touches all sides of the serving dish. Place briefly under broiler to bake the meringue a light brown.

Green Beans and Spaetzle

This economical main course was often served during the lean years of the late 1930s, but was also a family favorite. It was served most often during the summer months, when green beans were fresh and plentiful.

Spaetzle

1 egg
1/3 c. water
¼ tsp. salt
¾ c. flour

Mix all ingredients until well blended. Bring pot of salted water to boil. Place small amount of dough on edge of thin plate or on a wooden board that has been planed down at one end. With a knife, cut small pieces of dough off the edge of the board/plate into the boiling water. Repeat with remainder of dough until all used. Boil 10 minutes.

Beans

Trim one pound fresh green beans. Place in pot with enough water to cover half of beans. Bring to boil, then simmer for about 6 minutes. Drain and rinse under cold water.

Croutons topping

I cup croutons, either prepared or homemade
½ c. sweet butter, melted

Assemble by beginning with a layer of spaetzle, top with beans, then alternate another layer, finishing with spaetzle. Top with croutons, and pour butter over all.

Grieveh

For Jews who observed the dietary laws (*kashrut*), it was difficult to find fat or oil that was acceptable for cooking foods to be eaten with a meat meal. Butter was only usable for dairy meals, and lard, the most popular fat for the general population, was unacceptable for Jews since it came from pork. The solution was to render the fat from chickens or geese. Not only did this provide fat for cooking, it also resulted in delicious cracklings (the skin). A large supply of chicken fat was generally prepared for Pesach, and then used the rest of the year, augmented by more as needed.

Skin and fat from 1 chicken (the more fat, the better)
1 onion, peeled and sliced
¼ tsp. salt
1 c. water

Cut the skin and fat into small pieces. Place in large frying pan; add onion, salt and water. Bring to boil, then reduce heat and simmer until skin and onions turn brown. Stir occasionally so that browning occurs evenly. Be careful not to overcook or let skin stick to bottom of pan. Drain fat from solids. Remaining skin and onions may be eaten as is or mixed with two hard boiled eggs. Either, way, this is delicious spread on matzoh, hearty rye or pumpernickel.

Hamantaschen

This is the recipe my mother used for Hamantaschen; it's slightly richer than Oma's Purimkuechle and the pastry is baked rather than fried. It can also be shaped in other ways to make delicious Danish pastries. One of our favorite meals, a treat for us perhaps twice a year, was fresh Danish, served with hot chocolate. Amazing to be able to eat the fresh pastries to our heart's content!

Dough
4 c. flour
½ tsp. salt
½ c. sugar
2/3 c. butter, softened
3 eggs
1 envelope yeast, dissolved in
1 c. lukewarm milk

Filling
Raspberry jam
nut, raisin, cinnamon mix
almond filling, canned
prune filling: pureed prunes with
¼ tsp. cinnamon, juice of ½ lemon

Glaze
1 c. confectioners sugar
1 tsp. vanilla flavor
3 Tbsp. water

Mix dry ingredients. Add butter and eggs until well blended. Add yeast-milk mixture. Blend and then knead until the dough is smooth. Let rise until doubled in bulk, about 1 hour. While dough is rising, prepare fillings.

Preheat oven to 375 degrees. Punch dough down. Working with 1/3 dough at a time, roll out to about ½ inch thickness. Using a glass with about a 5 inch diameter or other round object such as a cookie cutter or empty can, cut the dough. Place 1 Tbsp filling in each circle. Fold up so that the pastry is in the shape of a triangle, and pinch shut. Place on baking sheet about 2 inches apart. Bake until light brown.

To prepare glaze, mix all ingredients to form a rather thin frosting. While pastries are still hot, brush with the glaze.

Italiano

The name of this salad suggests that it was considered somewhat exotic by my south German family, although it uses only familiar ingredients. At any rate, it was a great summertime favorite for us all and made the transition to the United States in tact.

3 large potatoes, boiled till soft, cooled and diced
2 eggs, hard boiled and diced
2 half sour pickles, diced
¼ lb. bologna, sliced and diced
6 pieces of pickled herring, diced
2 Tbsp. cider vinegar; more if desired
2 Tbsp. canola oil
Salt and pepper to taste

Mix all ingredients gently in a large bowl. Chill until ready to use, though best served at room temperature.

Lebkuchen

These cookies are traditionally made at Christmas, and seem to be the south German equivalent of the British fruit cake. Mama also made them in the winter, but for us they were a Chanukah delicacy. While Mama had the candy store, Lebkuchen were a standard and popular cookie among those she made for sale.

¾ c. honey
½ c. sugar
¼ tsp. salt
¼ tsp. baking soda
1 egg, well beaten
1 Tbsp. cocoa
1 tsp. cinnamon
1 tsp. cloves
1 tsp. rum flavoring
¾ c. chopped mixed glazed fruit
½ c. almonds, blanched and coarsely T chopped
3 c. flour

<u>Icing</u>
1 c. confectionary sugar
3 Tbsp hot water
¼ tsp rum flavoring

Preheat oven to 375 degrees.

Mix honey, sugar, soda, salt, egg, cocoa, cinnamon and cloves. Add flavoring, fruit and almonds. Add flour and stir until well blended.
Spread mixture on a jelly roll pan or cookie sheet with sides. Pat dough smooth with floured hands. Bake about 20 minutes, until lightly browned.
Blend sugar, water, and flavoring to make a soft, smooth icing. Smooth icing over hot surface of cookies. Cut while hot. Let cool on cookie sheet before removing.

Linzertort (Raspberry Tarts)

A standard delicacy in Kenzingen, raspberry tarts were made to mark all kinds of special occasions. They were served to honored guests, as holiday treats, and for birthdays. My Oma often had a tart reserved in case she had to bring special food to a funeral. Because they were made with butter and nuts, they aged very well and kept for rather a long time. It's also been a tradition in our family to mark the secular new year with a raspberry tart.

½ lb. butter or other shortening
½ lb. grated almonds
1 c. sugar
2 eggs (save 1 yolk)
1 tsp. baking powder
2 c. flour
2 Tbsp. whiskey
½ tsp. ground cloves
2 tsp. cinnamon
2 Tbsp. cocoa
½ tsp. salt
raspberry jam

Cream butter and sugar; beat in eggs. Stir in almonds and spices. Add remaining ingredients and blend well. If the dough is very soft, add another ¼ c. flour.

Divide dough in half. Spread 2/3 of the dough evenly in the bottom of a well-greased, 8 inch layer cake pan (preferably with a removable bottom). Spread raspberry jam over the dough, leaving the edges bare. Take reserved dough and roll into a long round roll, about ½ inch thick. Place some of the roll around the edge of the pan (keeping hands well floured is helpful). Take rest of roll to make a lattice pattern on top. Treat second half of dough in similar fashion; designs on top of jam can vary.

Bake at 350 for c. 30 minutes or until done. Let cool slightly before removing from pan.

Matzoh Dumplings

Matzoh balls are a favorite menu item among Jewish diners, not only during Pesach, but all year long. This variation is served specifically at the Seder meals, although Daddy loved to have the leftovers the next day for breakfast, fried in butter.

4 matzohs, soaked in warm water
4 eggs
1 tsp salt
2 Tbsp. oil
2 large onions, diced and fried
1 c. matzoh meal

When matzohs are soft, remove from water and squeeze out as much liquid as possible. Add to pan in which onions have been fried and sauté until mixture is quite dry. Remove from heat. Add salt and eggs and mix well. Add matzoh meal. Let rest at least one hour. If mixture still is too wet to form into balls, add another ¼ c. matzoh meal.
Bring large pot of salted water to a boil. Form matzoh mixture into balls, about the size of a golf ball. Drop into boiling water and let cook until tender (c. 15 minutes). Do this in batches of up to ten balls. Remove from water with slotted spoon and place into a greased baking pan. Continue until all the mixture is used up. Bake matzoh dumplings at 350 degrees for 45 minutes. Best served with gravy from brisket, chicken, or other meat.

Pear/Prune Kugel

This kugel is the south German version of East European cholent. It's a dish made on Friday that can be cooked overnight to be eaten hot on Shabbat. Since my Oma didn't have an oven capable of baking food slowly for a long time, she brought her kugel to the baker on the corner of her street, and he obligingly baked it overnight for her. It can be made with either prunes (which were cheaper) or pears that had been preserved by Oma and Mama the previous fall. We always considered this kugel a real treat.

½ lb. beef suet, cut into very small cubes
1 lge. or 2 med. onions, finely diced
1 tsp. salt
2 Tbsp. sugar
1 tsp. ground ginger
4 c. flour
¾ c. water
½ lb. prunes, stewed or
    1 lge. can pears in own juice

Mix suet, onions, and dry ingredients. Add enough water to make a semi-firm dough. Place in casserole dish and bake at 350 for 1 hour. Remove from oven. Pour liquid from prunes or pears over baked kugel. Arrange pears or prunes on top to cover entire surface of the kugel. Cover. Bake at 350 for 1-2 hours, or at 250 overnight. Check kugel after 1 hour; if kugel seems dry, add more juice from fruit and continue baking.

Potato Soup with Sausage

This was another popular meal in our home, and one that was quite economical. Obtaining kosher deli was difficult during the Nazi years, so this soup was a good way to stretch one sausage among the three of us.

4 Potatoes, peeled and quartered
6 c. water
2 med. onions
1 Knackwurst, halved lengthwise and thinly sliced

Cook potatoes in lightly salted water until soft. Mash coarsely in the water. Chop and fry onions in chicken fat until golden brown. Add to potato broth. Simmer for 15 min. Add knackwurst to soup and cook another 15 minutes.

Serve hot.

Purimkuechele

This is my Kenzingen Oma's recipe – it's a variation on the better known Hamantaschen that are traditionally eaten on Purim.

4 c. flour
½ c. butter
2 eggs
1 envelope yeast, dissolved in
1 c. lukewarm milk
½ tsp. salt
½ c. sugar
1 c. raisins

Mix all ingredients, except raisins, in a large bowl. Knead until the dough is smooth. Let rise until doubled in bulk. Punch down. Work raisins into the dough.
Using a 4 quart pot, fill half full of oil and heat to 375 degrees.
Break off piece of dough about size of a golf ball. Shape dough with hands into a roughly triangular shape. Drop into oil and fry until golden brown. Remove to paper towel to absorb excess oil, then sprinkle with sugar and cinnamon if desired. Best eaten fresh.

Sauerkraut and Mashed Potatoes

My Oma in Kenzingen always had a barrel of cabbage pickled each fall. Sauerkraut was a staple of winter meals and a way to ensure that we had vegetables in our diet even when fresh greens were unavailable. The fondness for sauerkraut was a legacy of our Alsace ancestors, and this dish is a typical Alsatian one.

4 potatoes, peeled, quartered, and boiled in salted water until soft.
1 onion, diced and sautéed in chicken fat until brown
2 c. sauerkraut.

Mash potatoes, then add onions and sauerkraut and mix well. If desired, more chicken fat may be added. Serve sausages (knackwurst) with this mixture.

Sweet and Sour Tongue

Most parts of a cow were used in our kitchen, as long as those parts were kosher. Thus, heart, lung, spleen and tongue were all served on a regular basis. Since most of these parts were generally considered less desirable, they were cheaper and a way to help stay within budget. Tongue, however, was considered a delicacy and therefore a real treat when it appeared on our table.

1 pickled tongue, boiled until soft, about 2 hours. Reserve broth.
While tongue is still warm, removed from broth, and peel off the skin that covers the entire tongue.
While the skinned tongue cools further, make the sauce:
2 Tbsp. oil
2 Tbsp. flour
2 cups of tongue broth, hot
1 tsp. ground cloves
3 bay leaves
3 Tbsp. brown sugar
3 Tbsp. cider vinegar

In a large skillet, over medium heat, make a brown roux: mix oil and flour and continue stirring until mixture is slightly brown. One tablespoon at a time, add the hot broth, mixing thoroughly after each addition. Mixture will at first be quite stiff, but will gradually become liquid. Once the mixture is liquid, remainder of broth may be added and thoroughly incorporated. Add remaining ingredients and stir to incorporate. Adjust sugar and vinegar to taste. Slice tongue and add to sauce. Let simmer for ½ hour. If sauce becomes too thick, add more broth as needed. Remove to serving dish and sprinkle with slivered almonds. Best served over egg noodles. (Remaining broth may be reserved and used as base for split pea soup.)

Breinigsville, PA USA
12 April 2010
235983BV00002B/3/P